MAYS 13

Varsity Publications Ltd

Varsity Publications Ltd
11- 12 Trumpington Street
Cambridge CB2 1QA

First published 2005 by Varsity Publications Ltd

This collection © Varsity Publications Ltd 2005

ISBN number 0 902240 36 6

Typeset in Garamond by Eve Williams
Produced by Cambridge Printing Park
Printed and bound in Malta

Original concept by Peter Ho Davies, Adrian Woolfson, Ron Dimant

All rights reserved. No part of this publication may be reproduced, stored in a retrieval system, or transmitted, in any form or by any means - electronic, mechanical, photocopying, recording or otherwise - without the prior permission of the Publisher.

A CIP catalogue record of this book is available from the British Library.

Further copies of this book and other titles in the series can be bought through all good bookshops or direct from *Varsity Publications Ltd.*, at the address above

www.mayswriting.com

Guest Editor	Robert Macfarlane
Editors	Jonathan Beckman Arthur House
Consulting Editor	Tom Marks

Sub-editors

Cath Duric	Victoria Hall
Paul Foote	Anouk Lang
Philippa Geering	Ross Mcelwain
Jenna Goldberg	Joe Moshenska
Kirsty McQuire	Zoe Organ
Kate Prentice	Tess Riley
	Ellie Simons

Publisher	Eve Williams
Cover Design	Katrina Beechey
Web Design	Tim Button

With many thanks to our college sponsors:
Cambridge: Trinity Hall, Sidney Sussex College, Christ's College, Pembroke College, Fitzwilliam College, Trinity College, Jesus College, Queens' College, Gonville and Caius College, Churchill College
Oxford: All Souls College, Trinity College

Natwest - Cambridge Branch

Thanks also to: Dr Michael Franklin, Pat Dalby, Joti Madlani, Dr Tim Harris, Helen Oyeyemi and especially to all at David Godwin Associates and everyone who submitted work.

Contents

POETRY

Balance james womack	*page*	6
Classmark AZN HPA R—CI DW paul foote		7
Gallery alexandra strnad		8
Gint boyd brogan		9
The Chimanimani 10k boyd brogan		10
Paint Terrace gerard o'donoghue		12
From the Modified Mercalli Earthquake Intensity Scale johanna celia winant		13
Sir Percival's Compassion john m cooper		14
Song jow lindsay		16
Tradescant's Rarities matthew sperling		18
Burn out this sepsis, trace... matthew sperling		20

PROSE

Sonnet Looking Back   22
zoe bullingham

Special Features   35
ned beauman

Boiling Water   42
joanna benecke

Good   46
nick mohammed

The Sleeping Faun   49
michael ledger-lomas

from The Tragedy of Beyoncé Knowles   57
jow lindsay

Here Be Dragons   70
leo shtutin

Threesome   73
ben morgan

The Fall of the St John-Hopkins   85
amir baghdadchi

The End of the World   101
fiona mcfarlane

INTRODUCTION

by Robert Macfarlane

First of all, some things that these poems and stories are not. They are not smeared in what Mark Twain once called "soul butter": that unguent mix of self-pity and self-righteousness which young writers in particular exude. They are not under the influence - are not obvious imitations of famous styles or authors. They are not exercises in weltschmertz; the hip ennui into which so much new writing lapses. And, finally, they are not tame or earnest, showing the plodding herd-think of writing which proceeds out of a dull sense of duty.

I start by declaring what these pieces are not, because there is little else which unites them, except their tonal ambitiousness, their urgency and their quality. Out of hundreds of submissions, the editors have sifted these twenty-one, and it is clear that they have chosen only with an agendum of excellence in mind.

"Tell the truth but tell it slant," wrote Emily Dickinson: there are so many angles of approach here. One thinks, among the poems, of the great tonal adventure of John M. Cooper's 'Sir Percival's Compassion', apparently a collaboration between Nietzsche, Monty Python and Julian Clary. It is a poem which is, unmistakably, on a quest for the burlesque - but which is also, in its odd way, seeking a vantage point of seriousness. It has its prose counterpart in Amir Baghdachi's 'The Fall of the St-John Hopkins', a headlong, hectic farce, driven full-tilt forwards by puns and idiocy and madcappery, utterly fluent in its own, utterly ludicrous, vernacular.

What a contrast those two make with James Womack's finely poised 'Balance', the poem which opens the anthology, and which plays such subtle games with the reader's equilibrium - or with Boyd Brogan's 'The Chimanimani 10k', a deft inspissation of the meterological, the political and the pastoral (those "velcro hills" snagging "cottonwool mists"). Then there is Matthew Sperling's 'Tradescant's Rareties', which unites, across time and through space, the differently futile efforts of two people to deal with the "random data" of experience, with the "qualia streaming slantwise around". Tradescant's prose partner would be, I think, the only historically inclined story in the collection, 'Sleeping Faun': narrated in a voice that is fey, louche, confident, and very sharp-eyed (watch for that "sweat drop" which "hatches" beneath the Reverend's curls).

I spoke of a tonal ambitiousness, and by this I meant the desire which is on display in many of these pieces to create new voices, almost new languages, for experience. Turn to Jow Lindsay's 'Song', for instance, and you find a lyric synthesised out of file names and SMS-gobbets ("it's too late/ & whatnot, & too foolish, & too fucked-up, but,/ I remember last night ,/ We watched the TV set.jpg together"), but which is still melancholically modern and beautiful. 'Song' sits alongside another strange, found poem, 'Classmark', which masquerades as a cento of one-liners randomly fossicked from library books, and whose magnificent ellided last line - 'Practice crashworthiness and the ocean floor' - hovers somewhere between eleventh commandment and flight-attendant's diktat.

Nabokov used to maintain that rhythm, the correctly ordered release of sound and stress within a sentence, was essential to the effects of his prose. He explained, too, that he worked arduously to find his tempo: a short sequence of words "often needed hours of effort before the rhythm was right, down to the last cadence, before the gravity of earth had been overcome". The master would have approved of many of the pieces here, both prose and poetry, in which such care has obviously been taken over rhythm. When you come to the sad, exquisite 'Gallery', for instance, make sure you read it aloud; and do the same for Sperling's 'The song, the varied action of the blood', and for Leo Shtutin's prose-poem-psalmic-epic, 'Here be Dragons', to hear the way in which it moves between the wheedling angsty voice of worry, through to a full vatic thunder ("let us all reproduce, for this is the era of parasites, this is the era of information, this is the era of the tick and of the leech").

And you must read out, too - even though it will take you a long time - Jow Lindsay's extraordinary 'The Tragedy of Beyoncé Knowles', for me the stand-out track of the collection. Truly strange, consistently weird (the best type of weirdness), it is a story in which - with its magnificently sassy one-liners ("his dimensions specified penis as his pussy of choice"), and its deep surreality (see Chapter 4 in particular) - Lindsay has created a new nadsat for the I-pod era.

I edited the May Anthologies in 1997, back when there were two Mays. It was the year Zadie Smith submitted sections from what would soon become White Teeth; I remember sitting with the other editors at the shortlist meeting, surrounded by empty pizza boxes and coke cans, our eyes out on springs at the preposterously brilliant standard of her submissions. Smith is only the most famous of the May debutants who have proceeded to literary renown. Agents now routinely scout the anthology for talent. This year again, readers - whatever their motives for reading - will not be disappointed

Robert Macfarlane's Mountains of the Mind (2003) won the Guardian First Book Award and the Somerset Maugham Award, among other prizes. He is a Fellow of Emmanuel College, Cambridge.

POETRY

james womack

Balance

It didn't want to let the morning
Come, as if the globe were rocking back
And forwards, gently swivelling like
A fair-day weathervane, and turning
Towards the sun, turning us away.
The world, calm but firm like a mother,
Did not allow it to be either
One thing or the other, night or day.
The sky was gritty with darkness, with
The light and the dark mixed, like the air
Was full of masonry-dust, plaster,
Powder, snowflakes, soot. I thought that if
I tore the page off the calendar
The next page would have the same number.
It didn't want to let morning come.
Fine by us. But the mechanism
Slips suddenly out of gear—we are
Jerked forward, lose balance once more.
This is Irkutsk station in autumn—
The sun is up, the scales have fallen.

paul foote

Classmark AZN HPA R—CI DW

The geology of chaos
                        sensa
   earth rocks of the river
(life of the group)
Plastic fractures and corrosion culture/boundaries
[edited by Sir Joseph D. Hooker]
Strength and fatigue as astrology
                        Switching
the mechanics of reminiscences and the
birth of classical strength
 Visions of the album—totality and the
        elasticity of the vibrations and
the resistance of matter

Stability for processing sickness
                (transmission and myth)
Practice the coordination of remote measurement
Practice crashworthiness and the ocean floor.

alexandra strnad

Gallery

Call me long-necked Botticelli lady love
lioness with the ropey trestles
dark smoky encrusted lashes
worn brittle by Venetian waters
pick me by my curve and snarl
paint me in oils curtain covered

Smelling of mildew a sodden gondola breathing in the canal belly bottom
down submerged street swimmer memorising touch paint scuffed scarlet
mouth and a marauder on your lower lip his backbone with its
triangular muscle waited clutching metal duodenum crush on the rib-cage
the spinal cord knots down and the wonder down beneath

Alabaster Madonna in mock-white
hair string silk on fire or coral patterns
when spread legged on his sheets
marble eyes aquamarine in hue
blink and search blink and hunt

Oh and just once more praise my sculptured skeleton sloping shoulder
unblemished flank feminine and pure untouched unsullied as yet unwept
Where impersonal breath steams my flesh eyes in tanks and sunglasses weep
Alone I am but warm in the oils my formaldehyde love encased timeless in
this wooden coffin frame.

boyd brogan

Gint

Over sweet tea and sour bread
the Abyssinian emperors
are much discussed. Menelik, Tewodros.

Building a wall: they hammer blocks
of concrete. The shards are tossed
in earth. Checked, sketchily replaced. They've freed

another truck. It growls down, mud
fresh on the hubs like womb-juice.
Staggering through ruts, a high-heeled horse.

The wall grows with an evenness
defiant of the accidents
of hammer, rock. Like coins in beggars' hands

Amharigna's *l's, g's, n's*
chink in the mouth. Char-black kettles.
A bar of soap wrapped in a leaf. Hot coals.

boyd brogan

The Chimanimani 10k
Cyclone Eline hit Chimanimani, Zimbabwe, in early 2000.

Cottonwool mists snagged on the velcro hills
disposable vapours, the airy litter
of careless gods: heavenly crisp-packets,
candywrap, ethereal fagbutts
discarded in disfiguring plantations
sodden sawmills, the dogged, down-at-heel
persistent threadbare scrub. Woodsmoke and rain
brand-new solid odours in a heavy air.

We arrived with the door falling off the kombi
held only by a leather trouserbelt
– the engine was a clanking random racket –
at nightfall: fifty klicks in seven hours.
Coming from the village, kerbcrawled briefly
through the peasouper by some rowdy drunk
we wondered about 'security', remembering
the dire prophecies at Bulawayo:
*The whole thing'll blow up in the next two weeks
- get out while you can.*
                But soon distracted
by this place's peculiar qualities
the way sunset was cloud-set, horizons
whitely approaching, maternal, sinister
like death in a bridegown. Night was a cloud
– walking in a fuselage of mist
cloaked in its silver lining, you'd believe
the whole dark areaplain in silent flight –
or, wandering out, you'd see the stars had dropped
to just a few metres, chandeliers
in a black ballroom.

Sure, the talk was all
politics: boozed-up late-night vehemence,
bewildering acronyms, the intimacy
of small-group confidences; CIO
and drugs cops made drunk quarrelsome visits;
'what part of NO does Robert Mugabe
not understand?' got scribbled on a menu:
US Peace Corps, VSO's discussed
the uncertain emergency procedures
over their chipped mugs of vodka-coke.

On Independence Day, a well-known flashpoint
I joined the 10k road race, finishing
well down a field of giggling highveld athletes
bemused by my redfaced clumsy efforts
but welcoming, no question. Two white farmers
had been shot, and unofficial roadblocks
postponed our drive to Harare that day.

But scrabbling up the tar with all the rest
- the guy in the *Mr Clean* t-shirt who won
and finished off the race with twenty pushups;
Jonah, the school champ but out of training;
the girls who all gave up, laughing, and walked –
such violent, unsuitable kids' tales
seemed risible as the idea of darkness
or cyclones, sweating in that clearskied sun
(though every hill was scarred with Eline's mudslides,
drying, since last month; and night would come).

gerard o'donoghue

Paint Terrace

In Horsham, a small brickhouse
garden backs against
the Pompey-Victoria track and
the terrace roars.

Strung across the aperture,
a sparrow-trap hangs, a
goal mouth to savour
the summer delicacies of
lob, volley and shot.

The express scream echoes
from painted throats,
races the gapes and is gone.

The silent roar goes on,
fading into childhood
with chipping paint and
heads or tails bets.

Each face is a Mum or a Dad.
A screamer stuck in the net.

johanna celia winant

From the Modified Mercalli Earthquake Intensity Scale (a sonnet)

Ten: Vibrations like an approaching truck.
Some objects — delicately suspended —
swing. At night, some awakened. Pendulum clocks
stop. Windows creak. Some furniture upended.
Then: The Love waves (that's what they're really called)
roll in. And rails bend, land slips, bridges shear.
Water overflows banks. Monuments fall.
Fissures seen in earth. Objects thrown in air.

"I felt the earth move." Can you say it straight?
Reread the octave. Is it an epic metaphor?
Do you buy it? Great sex may be that great,
but is love all collision, crash, no more?

No. I don't think love is the sensation
of violent motion, but slow rotation.

john m cooper

Sir Percival's Compassion

Tears and dew glistened in the Moon's sweating face:
Sunk almost, in Dawn's pale blue lips.
Two swollen violets' buds were his heavy eyes
Overcharged with rain, dashing down upon his breast
Their salty dew. Mists panted like breath,   5
Like the wolf's breath; Sir Percival loiters,
Resolved to love his boyish fear of solitude.
And so had he slumbered in sorrow that day,
But for the wanton cry amidst the Persian dawn:
          "Percival! Percival!,"   10
She said; she drew him from the friendly-threatening wood,
She said, "The sun spreads red amongst the æther:
The rocks are clotted, and the rocks are red;
Come to my bed, resist the day," and,
          "Percival, Come to my bed".   15
Elegantly supine, lounged on poppy flowers,
With a tent of fatuous flowing silks,
A lady let her corset fall,
And pressed her breasts against his chest.
Down by her naked he laid him down,   20
Down by her trembling, iridescent breast;
On it, the sun's red runes expressed
The bloody harvest of the morning.
(And by adventure, and by grace,
His sword lay naked on the earth)   25
"Now," she said, "shall you do with me what you will".
Moonlight pierced the air with pointed shafts,
And she sighed and she moaned
And he tasted of her sweating flesh.
The light which lit the body of the boy   30

Alit upon the unsheathed glistening hilt of his sword,
                "Percival! Percival!"
She said; she said, "Your god is dead".
Tearing her gorgeous body from him,
He grasped the flaming metal on the floor: 35
On his knees, held the blade tight to his torso,
And felt the steel burn its herald on his skin.
He saw the lady writhe and scream,
And the silks dissolve in roaring blasts
Of yelling, hell-bent winds.   40
It seemed the structure cracked, was torn away,
And on a chequered chapel floor, Sir Percival lay.
The lady's gone, the lover left,
With a bleeding spear, his thigh has cleft.
He bleeds at the dusty foot of the Cross, and cries to Christ: 45
"Take these bloody, bloody sheets, in recompense
Of that which I have misdone against Thee, Lord".
And his smarting wound bathes his boyish body,
Bathed bloody in the carmine light, spent
From a streaming stained glass chapel window,   50
Which crosses Christ's cross upon the floor.
His lonely fear roars around him like the wilder lion,
Quivering his flesh in fits—but a hand
Descends, brings a silver dish, and a crush of silk—
White and pure, the sash which slashed his shield—   55
And bloodies it, with the staunching of his wound.

jow lindsay

Song

when I was young it was fun,
we watched the train set together.tiff.
 & when it was later it was better,
we watched the rain wet the heather.tiff.

"lips, lips arc far along the stars.
the possibility of small print
is the full supple extent of it"þx.
I wake up with a yucky mouth
full of dreams
I wish I'd yell out,
but can't remember what they mean:

& when I was less young it was best,
 we watched the sun set.tiff, in the West
 (except once, which was odd),
& you a princess in that light.tiff,
 & I, God.*,
& at night you'd wield whips & wear leather.mov,
& I kissed your hand.avi & made a list of my demands.rtf:

& now that we're not, I think I've forgot,
 or tell what I remember in a ramble.arc,
sets of dentures.jpg, I think we've watched,
 but morning eyes hatch weary scramble.jpg,
& I forget, I forgot, adventures fade,
 it falls to Fate.* to guess which bits she made up,
& what I made up, but it's too late,
 & whatnot, & too foolish, & too fucked-up, but,

I remember last night,
 we watched the TV set.jpg together,
 because it sank to the hills.jpg & shone on the river.jpg
  & covered it all in Seinfeld.jpg in silver.jpg,
& the light.jpg seemed familiar.tiff,
 so I kissed your brow & made a vow.bat,
  as if I'd ever never.*.
I kissed you.* & I vowed to you.
 *.

matthew sperling

Tradescant's Rarities

John Tradescant (ca.1580-1638) came from Meopham in Kent – the village I grew up in – to be the greatest collector, traveller and naturalist of his age, gardener to Charles I. Tradescant the Younger (1608-62) succeeded him. Their collection of rarities, 'The Ark' in Lambeth, passed to Elias Ashmole and so formed the basis for the Ashmolean Museum, Oxford. The poem begins outside the museum: St. Giles.

This traffic. These arrivals. Every atom (which is the smallest
indivisible unit of time) shows cars, green lights, the street, that blanket
      I stumbled when I saw

                —that red, discarded pair of rubber gloves
                for spooling bitumen or tarmacadam
                lying in the gutter looks
                like a dead bird smashed on a window,
                      almost

      Nothing
is apropos: flux and reflux come and dissolve, in-
solubly
        while John Tradescant, the keeper
          of gardens, vines and silkworms, the *senex*
                    puerilis, the boyish
                  old man in his finery,
hoarding his queer *naturalia* (all these
minimal lilies, the hawk-gloves of monarchs, Chief Powhatan's mantle,
encephalitic or Siamese foetuses pickled in vinegar, labelled
LUNATIC BABY), tells us *Natura nihil*
agit frustra, Nature
        does nothing in vain. From the Ark,

at least a nucleus of the less perishable
items has survived:

broken jars, fragments
of crockery, ampoules of morphine, clumps
of congealed paint

—uncanny, faced with this mockery (say it, *a marriage
of monkeys*), where the excess of the actual might
be reduced
        might be calcined: to quicklime,
to vapour. Where objects refuse to be held,
they won't, they won't be themselves: random data, their qualia,
streaming
slant-wise around me, now troping themselves   in the
                                      turning confection.

matthew sperling

the song, the varied action of the blood

Burn out this sepsis, trace
   the line the vein
describes until it reaches
   lymph-nodes, lodes
of crude health to be exploited,
   worked, refined,
now filigreed, now hammered
to a *fleur-de-lys* ringing with good
   broken music, veins and chambers
coursing with an elixir – Lucozade
   Sport – oh my chevalier!

         The moment hangs, prolonged
in the failing body. Returns
   diminish; the fire
gutters and recedes. The song
takes as its measure what the song
   desires.

Prose

Sonnet Looking Back

He wasn't Tia then. At least, not everywhere you look. Not on supermarket billboards, hugging power-tools. Not on TV, offering the advice of a past winner to the oozing wannabes of *Snap Crackle Pop*. Not in *Gob* and *'Ere!* and *Brazen Chic*, or whatever those flimsy weeklies are called that cover the cigarette burns on NHS coffee tables. Particularly that picture of him performing high above stage in a hammock, his stilettos dangling wantonly over the edges.

He was Sonnet. Full name Jay Sonnet, but he'd been known by his surname since childhood. He'd been a bony and shrill child, with the impulses of a kamikaze Chihuahua. He'd bounded to the defence of trapped flies, equal opportunities for girls on the football pitch and the violently striped wardrobe (which he copied) of band *Mine's The Artic Groove*, giants of little-known genre 'keyboard kitsch'. To relax when not defending, he'd urged melodies from the sickbay's reluctant piano, or hummed them to the fields from halfway up the abbey pylons. Since childhood, then, his surname had seemed like Godsent permission to take the piss.

At fifteen, self-consciousness had awoken in him - like most things late, melodramatically. Mortified that all his friends were earnest, well-groomed girls who didn't fancy him, he'd slicked shapes of mischief into his hair and adopted the worldly drawl of a concrete-mixer attendant. This did not win him respect from the sultans of his own gender, as he'd hoped. In fact, they scorned his use of their mannerisms as they might a vicar who thought a tuxedo made him a libertine. So there came no invitation to slump with the boy-racers around the derelict swimming pool on Moxley Avenue. To holler with them there about what great throbbing stereos they had and what great throbbing cocks, all the better to pound you with, Little Red Riding-Whore, whichever sullen barmaid she was that week.

By the time school had done its gargling and spat him out,

Sonnet had re-settled comfortably into the outskirts of his own gender. He'd resumed his natural burble, reduced his hair sculptures to one exclamatory quiff and was no longer ungrateful for growing up different. It made him unafraid to be different now, faced with the future slopped out like prison dinners to the shoddy-lettered in that town: boy-racer becomes stock-replacer becomes chain-smoking betting-shop pacer. If you made it into middle-age at all. Graffiti on the Gruffudd bridge had once read: IS IT A BIRD - IS IT A PAIN - OR ARE YOU JUST A FUCKIN LEMMING. The Samaritans had nailed a sign over it, suggesting you call them before you jump.

Sonnet resolved that was not the life for him.

At night, the town's horizon was jagged with the silhouettes of its industrial fire-escapes. Below this rusting canopy teemed kebab carrion; the reeling disaffection released by Happy Hour; dealers delivering their goods to doorsteps immersed in milk bottles; and policemen scratching their *Insta-Mint* scratch-cards, stitches or genital warts. At night in such a town, business was strong for taxis. It was in its taxi industry that I met Sonnet in his early twenties, two years ago.

Roadrunner Taxis was manned from an ex-warehouse. Small businesses went round and round like hamster wheels there, attempting to get off the ground. A lifetime's supply of Stiff Nipple Jokes came free with each office, courtesy of the Alaskan ambience. Lower floors also got spiders in deathbed embraces with teabags deep in the tin.

Founder of *Roadrunner* ("*Meep meep!* Don't you watch Looney Tunes, skip-for-brains?"), central fixture in its office and mystic on its airwaves was Maxine. She was proud to have broken through "the wall of sagging testicles" said to preserve the top jobs in the taxi industry for "tweedy dodge that's got one cigar from used cars, another from internet porn and another they keep safe because it's been up the local Lewinsky". She was careful, however, to consider those who might dismiss her sex appeal because she wanted equality in the workplace. So every day she garnished and cooked her hair until it was an aromatic cascade of muddy blonde. She would hurl it all back and gurgle a dirty
laugh, going for porn star. She managed pirate.

It was Maxine who called me to announce I had been specially selected to helm one of her night chariots. This would putter to the aid of decaffeinated businessmen and clubbers whose boots were held together by safety-pins; none of them sure how much money, love or future they had. Passenger-driver empathy then came as standard.

The experience went like this. Whole hours sat 'banked at the rank', watching clouds pile up above the buildings lit like pumpkins in the darkness. Then life tumbling into the backseat to remind me of itself and give me ten minutes of purpose. My world shrank to an asphalt arrow, neon and speed warnings smearing in its margins as I hurled my whole soul into delivering the perfumed heap to the poker game without 'giving him motion sickness', or the old aged pygmy back home before the carton-milk got too warm for her cat. She with no better sense of what time it was than she had of the cat's death six months ago.

Sonnet was a fellow driver. At no point did he turn and sizzle himself into my consciousness with his eyes the colour of moist teabags. I noticed him only when he nudged me rather plaintively and announced he'd been there since my first day on the job. I took one of his Marlboros and his word for it.

He'd swing over from his cab and drape himself broodily in the window of mine like a policeman who might turn out to be a stripogram. But short men can't drape. He'd bend his smile into gigolo shapes. But his smile was naturally boyish - so the result was facial yoga: the beginner's class. He'd strike matches off his watchstrap like a badass motherfucker. But he took his mother shepherd's pie in Tupperware every weekend. His meanest was to look preoccupied during her sentimental re-enactments of the illnesses she'd brushed with that week.

It seemed, then, his machismo still busked at full force in the presence of a 'fit' woman (he kept trying this on me in different voices as though it were an 'open sesame'). He accompanied this with enough *Pharaoh SX* body spray to set dogs barking. It all said VIRGIN in tawdry neon lights. My loins remained at room temperature.
Thankfully, I was a deft hand in Cupid's kitchen and knew ways of cooling the fat of an attraction without causing spatter.

I introduced a hint of that 'freshly wrenched from the jaws of a dog' look to my clothes and hair. I gave him eye contact only as cursorily as I would the tattooed architect of a cheap cut and dry. I talked about breath mints, a selection of that week's roadworks and Welsh politics. When not talking, which I ensured was rare, I framed my state dentistry in a gawp.

He took about the average time to peel the wishful thoughts from his eyes. There was a final frenzy of invitations to drink in his back garden, with its town-renowned view of the hilltop they filmed on in *Felony Come Home*. Then his attentions tapered to twitchy silence like dying cicadas.

And so our future was as mates, paddling a lukewarm life together without abashment at our ingrown toenails. Even if I did still sense a certain knightly gravitas in his company. I let it be because his chivalric code seemed only to consist of keeping me in peppermint gum.

So it was, until he invited me to watch him perform.
Two years before, Sonnet had tipsily jounced into the fairy lights of the Karaoke Night at his local. This was a biker's brooding-ground, where the souls were as leathery as the clothing. A curious symptom of this was that nine out of ten preferred smoochy-pop on the jukebox. They therefore welcomed Sonnet's resurrection of his childhood favourites, not quite throwing their knickers at him but certainly grunting first prize his way. He went back every week and repeated his triumph until he'd won enough to buy a keyboard.

Since then, with his shadow mocking his every move on the garage walls, he'd churned out and refined his own electronic confectionery. This led his sister to scratch on the door at two am and hand him a watermelon stabbed with a bread knife. It also led to a weekly slot at a downtown cabaret.

Club Mesmerex was crouched between warehouses as though to grimace at its reflection in the April puddles. Inside, I saw a bar backed by a red-light district of smudgy neon beer ads. I saw lava lamps burbling like lewd gossip amidst plastic jungle undergrowth. I saw chintzy-tied businessmen spreading their crotches and schoolgirls inscribed with *'Cuddles n' Cream'* spinning like flies from knee to knee. I saw Maxine, but pretended not to.

When I saw Sonnet, it appeared there was something he had neglected to prepare me for.

A janitor with the air of a born-again Christian shambled onto the stage to needle a frown through the punters. He muttered, "Yep. Tia," into the mike. The audience applauded as limply as if they'd been fanning themselves with magazines for four hours. Except for Maxine, who rattled the ice in her rum and howled, "Roll it *onnn*".

Over the drinkers settled a hush both electric and sheepish. Then a spotlight stabbed the stage curtains, and out of them, as they parted, slunk a stiletto.

I had been roughing up a complimentary bowl of pockmarked olives with a toothpick. A few suddenly abandoned ship and paddled out radially across the spillage on the bar. Maybe something to do with me. I can't be sure of that or anything in the few seconds it took for the sight onstage to kindle in my veins.

The velvet gown was that shade of purple Cleopatra might favour for her lingerie. The russet tresses of the wig were pinned up in a swirl at the back of his head, then skewered with flamingo feathers. His eyes were smutty with mascara and with the tease oozing out of their corners. His lipstick was sticky nectarine. The dunes of muscle in his bared shoulders were not so pronounced as to forego the aesthetics of tender power. The tricks of the light and of the corset hyped the breasts to an unobjectionable volume. The legs were short, and pale as the eyeball sky of the Welsh town that had nurtured them, with its flora that hung its head like its lawyers for lack of light to lean towards, and its summer that was its spring with more toads and more car accidents. But they were sleek,
gymnastic legs, with the generous slit in the gown licking the left thigh up and down as he moved. Flicking out a backward lash of velvet as he switched from slinking one way to another. Rippling with the sultry rhythms of his pre-recorded keyboard accompaniment.

Meanwhile he sang the lugubrious *Choose To Lose*, his voice knotted with desire, like someone too drunk to make love. There was no falsetto. The huskiness of the voice only boosted the sexual pathos of the performance, suggesting this kinkily walking wounded of too many smouldering midnights was also one of too many consolation cigarettes.

He finished by offering his lips for a kiss from the audience. Then the curtains swept across, swift as a middle-class hush across a breakfast table that has noticed a lovebite.

The audience applauded as dizzily as if they'd been slapping themselves with magazines for four hours. I remained a rigid twist with a toothpick in the shadows, daring no public display of what I felt inside.

My applause went deeper than my hands. I had been pulsing with it from the very first slink.

Sonnet soon appeared at the bar, still in costume - in the interests of rapid fluid replacement or just flaunting it, I couldn't say. This was an all-new bundle of virtues and vanities before me.

He saw me, smiled, and I flinched. A crossroads smile.

Had a bucking horse been near, I would have leapt on it. To hell with injury and humiliation. Such a straddling might also have brought relief where I suddenly needed it.

Our surroundings were decidedly lacking in horses. So I bought Sonnet a gin and tonic (overruling his request for lager) and clunked it with mine on a secluded banquette. Up close, the breasts were reminiscent of the palm-sized pimples anorexics get when they trade flesh for widespread desire for it. On stage, someone blew their life story through a saxophone.

I said very little, moved even less, and let my eyes graffiti it all over him. I had no pretensions - this riot in my blood wasn't poetry. Actually, I had no idea - this riot in my blood was exactly that; my mind was bound and gagged in the closet.

Meanwhile, Sonnet babbled. It had started a few months ago, he said, during a kitchen spat with his sister over how crumby was too crumby for smearing excess margarine back into the tub. He'd noticed her knee boots forlorn on the linoleum and leapt into them, hoping his dirty feet would have her crying surrender. When this failed, he'd strutted about in them, impersonating a fat lady singing that it was over. And so he'd arrived at his Unique Selling Point.

His sister did his costumes now and was that one over there, sniffing her margarita suspiciously. His USP was: drag without the fag inside. Because he wasn't gay, you see (I slalomed a fingertip down his arm and Marilyned, "Show a girl...?" He blinked, blushed and generally spurted confusion like a malfunctioning car-wash. I snapped a matchstick between my fingers and resumed a knotted silence). As for his stage name, he'd snatched that from a bottle in his sightline on the night of his first performance ('Maria' had been obscured by the barman's thumb).

He was drawn to the range and intricacy of female costume. And, more than that, to toying with the cock-strings of the mainstream swagger-boys, who'd go home and grind at any available vagina to emphasise that no frock tricks had excited them. Not that swagger-boys were often among the audience here. These were all fusty moths to a late licence, or to anonymous hubbub fit for brooding whisky-eyed on lost youth or a bra-strap. It was only (he smirked) a few old dodgers in the corners who openly clotted with lust.

I decided I didn't like him talking.

I suggested he accompany me to the toilet. He denied needing to go. I suggested he accompany me to a worthwhile place that had, for the sake of the disorientated, TOILET on its door. He looked disorientated. I took his satin-gloved hand; I took him for a walk.

The Ladies was empty when we entered. I kept it that way by thrusting Sonnet back against the door. It was then that he understood and went from giddily limp to giddy-up-and-take-me limp.

I closed my eyes and began to wrench relief out of him, focussing on those areas that took his breath away or trapped it inside him. I wanted him silent as a mannequin.

His flesh was raspberry-soft on my tongue, shapely as a bosom in my mouth. My fingertips rampaged over a sinuous terrain of velvet. I corrected him when he attempted to slither out of the gown. Again when he started picking at my bra-strap like a housewife at a fuse box. I diverted his fingers to my hair and saw to foreplay myself by shimmying my breasts against his corset. Soon I was using the full length of him for friction of this kind. Then he was raising the slit in the gown all the way up his thigh, and offering his only contribution of any note.

I accepted it almost incidentally, without opening my eyes.

Success came, and forcefully, only by keeping his offering in but Sonnet himself out of it.

In my unease afterwards, it was even more hastily than I'd rumpled it that I smoothed our clothing, before backing out of his personal space. I stood to attention at the tampon machine, as though it had made me do this and I was now awaiting further instructions.

Meanwhile Sonnet picked cigarette butts out of a sink, dizzily twisted its taps and flopped his face in to smile underwater.

Too sweet an opportunity. I sidled out of the door.

With my head bowed, I cut through the club and out into night.

Eleven months later, long after I'd moonlighted to Blackpool with a black-market permit to sell ice-cream, I received a call from *Szzzle*.

This was a magazine prescribing celebrity fawning as self-esteem Polyfilla for everyone else. Their budget covered looking me up on Google, but not dispatching a nodding doll with a Dictaphone beyond London. They had demonstrated similar journalistic grit in the feature they had already run on my relationship with Tia when he was a hardening twinkle in the big time's eye. An uncredited Kodak of me fish-facing against the window of a bus-stop accompanied titbits of local testimony confirming I dyed my hair 'promiscuously' and had a 'chilli pepper mouth' sure to sour any childhood in earshot.

Szzzle had now advanced to the personal touch, calling with their pencils erect for my reaction to new rumours.
It was alleged that Tia and I had parted after two months because of an itching libido that no one of two nether-holes could nurse. One need only consider, Szzzle suggested hypnotically, Darcy Snow: Tia's rival in *Snap Crackle Pop* and a homo 'lite' who took his multi-vitamins and his mother seriously. Those crackling silences between Darcy and Tia in the house shared at night by the contestants! Darcy's reference to "the telltale tear in your dress" in *Apocalypse In My Coffee Cup*, the 'ballad of common love' he'd written and performed shortly before losing out to Tia in the final round!

I took the call with sunset clustering around my office skylight like a celestial *hush*. Recalcitrant tubs of *LipLix Whipple* had made way for a secretarial position at an adoption agency specialising in Estonian infants and in squinting when it came to paperwork. I was as idle-blooded as ever. My pulse got no perkier at *Szzzle*'s approach - I had moulted this skin, they could do what they wanted with it. But it was with someone else in mind, and something higher rumoured in that sunset, that I used my steady hand to raise the bullshit hose.

I told *Szzzle* that a homo tends not to make a plump schoolgirl his bathwater, bath-towel and mouthwash - all to limber up for me, rustling in ache for him in the bedroom. I told *Szzzle* my dying Catholic mother (truth) had asked me to put a baby in her arms before she entered God's garden (truth-ish – she'd asked for the Egyptian crockery I'd pawned at seventeen). My relationship with Sonnet had ended because he'd insisted the overruling destiny of his loins was to kinky-twist onstage (I mentioned Dido and Aeneas. *Szzzle* got sniffy and assured me her ex-fiancé was called Matt). I told *Szzzle* to go smoke the photo they claimed they had of "Pop sensation Tia breaking the news of his sexuality to me in the parking lot of Wales's leading beauty salon".

After that, I was small news again.

So I never got to tell them that two months is how long I could keep Sonnet as a human sex toy. Advantage: no risk of flat batteries on a Sunday night when nowhere was open but the motorway services twelve miles away. Disadvantages: powered by feelings of its own; comes with verbal ability as standard. Every Saturday night, I frocked him up and rode him all the way to kingdom come. Then I buried him in the bottom drawer of my attention again. He was expected to remain inanimate until I next required him. Two months is how long he could take it.

He said he wasn't a fag, but that is how I thought of the two options offered to me after that night at *Club Mesmerex*. In one hand, I could settle for just the one; in the other, take a packet and maybe a habit too. My soul was full of tar already. But passive to my selection was Sonnet, freshly lolloped into my arms, his soul pink and tender as a koala's earlobe.

Just the one might cause him temporary shortness of breath and disorientation, but nothing in the long-term. It meant explaining that, because of my dying Catholic mother, I had been emotionally dizzy that night. Winking some joke about having borrowed his walking stick. Then an apology, and assurance it wouldn't happen again.

The packet might prove emotionally cancerous. It meant explaining I'd left *Mesmerex* so hurriedly to take a mobile call from my dying Catholic mother. Then suggesting I drive him back to mine for dinner after his next performance.

I took a few days off for detox, as was my custom after a one-night-stand. I pinned together the curtains of my bedsit for an appearance of long-term absence. In the accompanying long-term dusk, I did yoga and Dostoyevsky, ready to contort myself around the shanks of my furniture in the style of an autistic cat at the trill of my mobile phone (I could never just turn it off - had to let it ring out and scold me). It never came - promising.

But a girl's got to work.

And all too soon Sonnet had his paws up on my cab windowsill. In his eyes was empty bowl. In his outstretched hand was peppermint gum.

Driving Tia home after his performances at *Mesmerex* was like hurtling an egg back to my lair. The challenge was to get it back while it was still warm from the mother without the chick breaking out - Sonnet. With his kitchen-sink 'introspection' demonstrating that he just didn't get it: if I welcomed only the barest necessity when it came to baring his body, I certainly didn't want him baring his soul. With the glow-in-the-dark plastic stars of adolescent admiration in his eyes, lit for five minutes by a single ray of kindness. With his hand hooked around his seatbelt like a paperboy holding the strap of his delivery bag.

Dinner was afterwards. Very much a *crinkle-snap-dinner is served* affair, but pleasant in its atmosphere of silent, sulky exhaustion. Among my most enduring memories of Sonnet are those half-hour meals in my bedsit. Backs against the boxes I'd never unpacked; legs stretched out towards the imprint in the carpet of a spread-eagled man, like a chalk silhouette from a crime-scene. Me in my underwear; Sonnet finally permitted to loosen his costume a clasp or two. On all sides, an electrically jewelled night where the world crouched for cover from what it had spawned by day; between us, a comfortable nothing.

If you wanted to do me a favour, you could say it was I who encouraged Sonnet to polish his act to a stellar level by rewarding powerful performance with mattress applause. No one wanted to do me a favour. His sister pushed me face-first under the hand-dryer of the *Mesmerex* toilets and growled into the ear that wasn't full of hot air that if she could "cock-lock the fool against me," she would. Then there was Maxine. She continued as normal to crackle with invective at the "cheek" of local pigeons/traffic lights/tax inspectors. But I saw the gossip fairy flitting in her eyes as she looked at me. Finally, I called in on her office for my third overdue paycheque, and we were alone. Apart from her central temple of Taiwanese power-toys, the only interruption to the carpet's violet diatribe against class was a filing cabinet. Maxine waited until I'd lowered my neck to it before asking if I was a lesbian. I bucked. Then I quipped rather savagely why "anyone would bother with dough when there was microwave cockery". She hadn't understood. Presumably why she'd looked to my breasts for footnotes.

Then, one night at *Mesmerex*, a talent scout had sidled in as I was propelling Sonnet towards my car. He represented Channel 11's *Snap*

Crackle Pop, and curtly suggested Sonnet enter the regional heat, finishing with a smoke-ring to emphasise the hip and fleeting nature of the opportunity. It was shortly after then that the glow-in-the-dark stars began to peel from Sonnet's eyes. He became paler and stiffer on my bedsit floor, making his contribution with all the passion of a man doing press-ups. At best, those press-ups were as though at the boots of a sadistic superior, and he performed them with a spirit of resistance - he would not be broken; his body could do cheap if that's what I wanted, because his soul was not mine, was not mine. On one such night, he'd
shaken his head with the force of a shiver and quietly observed I was interested only in fetish-fuck with someone he was not.

I'd thrown a stick for him to chase into the bushes. I'd asked: was he not himself, then, on stage? He said: more there than anywhere. Well then, I'd snorted. He'd looked hopeful, but dizzily.

I could not have denied wanting Tia without the Sonnet inside. Without all his peeping through his costume with his hopes of The Small-Town-Couple Experience. Windswept mornings throwing crab apples at the beer cans bobbing like mutant fish in the canal. Smoky afternoons at a lopsided bar, hands cuffed around our glasses of anaesthetic to the ordinary. Salty evenings wandering the dank walkways between the fever-eyed special offers at *Aquaworld*. Perhaps those visions could somehow have slid into being despite ourselves, were it not true that every Hearts he'd pulled out in conversation had met with a Spades from me – long after that had stopped being intentional, to encourage him to put his mouth to other uses.

Our last night together had static in its folds from the start. Sonnet had out-purred twelve other contestants to win a place in the regional final of *Snap Crackle Pop* the following week. With his success he took on a sharpening air of caffeine and finger-snap. Meanwhile, I'd accepted we had nothing to talk about and wanted only tenderness - of the inflicted-by-runaway-passion variety.

He was compliant throughout the act itself. After he'd dressed (repouched his groin), he stood by the window and its blushes of neon rebounded in blades from his leather knee-boots. Traditionally, at this point, our silent, sulky dinner began. Instead, he turned and growled he was "not just a sex object, you know". My eyes went for a spin. I suggested he stop being such a girl.

A flurry of colours crossed his face. None of them would have looked amiss in a bruise.

Then he'd snatched up his handbag and been a man. No looking back, no braying phone call, no box of *Comforts* from the petrol station. I liked him more in that moment than any other.

Where Sonnet's story went after ours splintered, I can be no more certain than any other *Szzzle* reader. He won the regional final, of course, then the televised national contest that summer. *Fell To Pieces (But Not In Your Back Yard)*, B-side on his second single, is said to address our break-up - I scratched the CD so it wouldn't play beyond the title track. He likes to drape his fiancé on buffalo rugs for *Chez Celeb* pull-outs. Some dimpled suburban truffle with principles as pristine as tennis whites and a libido as straightforward as a ballboy's.

My dying Catholic mother cannot help me now, as an excuse or otherwise. I was shaken when my brother the pious publican 'mentioned' she hadn't liked the way I'd turned out - because what she'd known of me was the hype. Stories of a nomadic career in PR that I'd fed to her on the silver tray of Conqueror envelopes and served with lavish cheques. I had been proud that I was not perched on her foot stool again, confessions leaping out of my mouth like lemmings. That I had not rattled her as her skeleton turned to scaffolding around the ruins of leukaemia and her memories melted in her eyes. I could not watch her memories melting in her eyes.

I wonder if Sonnet will still be among mine when they melt that way. At the moment they keep circling back, like street dogs sniffing a pigeon corpse, to Maxine. Hurling back her cascade of muddy blonde to gurgle her dirty laugh; looking to my breasts for footnotes.

There is an insistence in the Blackpool lights that makes it harder to leave your troubles to be smothered by cobwebs here. I try anyway. I binge on pictures of his squealing female fans: evidence you can be straight and fancy him. I let a few truckers at my lap and cry out to be told that I like this.

Then I go and spoil it all by thinking of Sonnet when he was fifteen. Slicking shapes of mischief into his hair and adopting the worldly drawl of a concrete-mixer attendant. Such transparent weakness, this dressing up of the true self in fear of the forest outside the campfire. And my dressing up of someone else? *In the same fear*, my thoughts mutter, and I shake them out of my head, and *in the same fear*, my thoughts mutter. In my insistently electric days, I hear a dirty pirate laugh from a hollow of weakness I never thought I had.

    Yesterday I bought *Mama Tia*, his special edition DVD, for the restless nights. Because everyone has a dirty habit.

ned beauman

Special Features

Transcript of Howard Benitz's audio commentary track on the DVD of City of Innards (2004)

Uh, hello, I'm Howard Benitz, and I'm going to be talking about my movie, City of Innards, which I wrote and directed. Actually it wasn't originally going to be called City of Innards, I was going to call it Autumn's Redemption, but the studio - oh, look, there's my name. Benitz with a ''z'. A lot of people get that wrong.

The movie opens with a sex scene because I wanted to really grab the audience's attention. In the leather harness there, that's Stephanie Willow, she plays Audrey - uh I mean uh Liz. Audrey was our wonderful creative consultant. My old friend Audrey. No, the character's called Liz. Steph said she would have been willing to show a lot more here but we had to think about the rating. I might have taken a few tapes of the outtakes home for my own private collection, ha ha! I'm joking, of course. I'm, uh, joking, Stephanie. That's Jimmy Conrad, he plays the police commissioner. Thrust away, Jimmy. Now, here, we didn't mean for the nipple to actually touch the camera lense, but by the time we noticed it was too late to go back and reshoot. Still, I think you can really see the influence of Bertolucci. Steph gets so much across with her acting here. We had some scenes written where Steph's character talks about her life, and in the end we couldn't afford to shoot them, but we would have learnt that she's had a lot of boyfriends, a lot of big-shots, a lot of handsome, charming, successful guys, but she's never been happy because really she wants someone, maybe, a little more sensitive, with a little more of, uh, an artistic temperament.

After the sex, here, where Jimmy's character eats a handful of raw mince, that was meant to show that he's kind of a caveman, and also to, uh, foreshadow his eventual death. Pure Truffaut. Now - there's dialogue, do I talk over the dialogue? I guess if you want to listen to the dialogue you can turn me off. He's telling her how there's been a lot of unexplained deaths in the city recently and how he's in a lot of trouble with the mayor. And now we show what he's talking about. A dark night - a guy running - a dog looking sort of surprised - some guys in hoods - and a scream.

Now we meet Rick, the hero of the movie, played by the brilliant Evan Shuke. Here he is in the library, researching ancient religions and demons and stuff. Audrey helped a lot with the development of this character. Actually Audrey helped a lot with the whole movie, I couldn't have done it without her. I met Audrey in college, we had some classes together, we were really good friends. She even stole my room-mate, ha ha! Yeah, after college I got an apartment in downtown LA, where I still live, and back then I was living with my buddy Dave. She used to hang out with me at the apartment a lot, and of course she met Dave, and before I knew it her and Dave were together! They were a nice couple. So they got engaged, and he moved in with her. Sadly, uh, things didn't work out, and she moved to Sacramento, and we didn't keep in touch as much as I would have liked, but then when I was about to start on City of Innards I got her number and called her up and asked if she wanted to be my creative consultant. I remember Audrey was so pleased that I was finally making a real movie, but she still took some persuading! But I brought her round, and I'm glad I did. I made sure she was there for every day of the shoot. Every day up until, uh, when she left. And the rest of the crew were great, too. Great people. And the cast. Particularly Stephanie. We had some good times. But all of them...I think Dave is a lawyer now.

So now we get our first look at the monster. I'll tell you a secret: in the first draft of City of

Innards, or, uh, as it was then called, Autumn's Redemption, there wasn't even a monster! Yeah, would you believe it? There weren't any voodoo cultists either. And even when I first introduced the monster, it played a pretty symbolic role, more as an aspect of Rick's psyche than anything else. It was more ambiguous. There really wasn't anything about human servants sculpting it, uh, a crude bride out of a giant pile of intestines and offal. The movie had more of a romantic, introspective slant, I suppose. It concentrated much more on the relationship between Rick and Liz. But when I was first in talks with the studio about them financing the movie, they had a lot of useful input, they were actually the first studio to take an interest in my vision as a director, and maybe this is a different movie to the one I intended to make all those years ago, but that doesn't mean it's... I mean, I don't think it's lost the metaphorical... That's actually Jimmy Conrad in the monster suit. We used some tricks with perspective to make him look really big. I'm sure you notice the echoes of Fellini here.

And by this point I was definitely trying to ramp up the suspense. Things have moved pretty fast. Here's Rick tied up by the cultists in his apartment, which, uh, is actually my apartment. I remember Audrey was surprised that we were shooting there. Actually she was surprised enough that I was still living there, ha ha! She stayed in the spare bedroom, Dave's old bedroom, while she was working on the film, which I suppose might have been kind of strange for her. She said, wouldn't be easier to shoot on a studio set? But I told her, you know, it's free, it's quiet, it's furnished, we don't need a permit, we don't have to deal with anyone complaining about the camera guy's muddy shoes, so... Here's Liz coming to see Rick so he can tell her what he's found out about the cultists. She knocks on the door - they open it - they've got her - they're holding her down and taking her clothes off - Rick's pet cat looks sort of surprised - they're letting the mutant out of the cage. Wow! Even I get excited watching this. Again, that's Jimmy Conrad in the mutant suit. A lot of people were confused about what exactly the connection was between the enormous monster and all these mutants. Maybe that's something to explore in the sequel.

This was kind of a distressing scene to shoot, where Rick in the next room has to listen, powerless, as, uh, the mutant rapes Liz over and over again. The studio said I ought to make her look like she was enjoying it at least a little bit, otherwise it would be too, you know, bleak. I'm glad they let me make my own call on that one. Some great acting from Evan, here, as Rick. He really captures what it feels like to... uh... Look how much he conveys with that facial expression, even under the gag and the fake bruising.

Yeah, this scene is pretty long.

OK, now Rick escapes from his captors. The fighting here took a long time to do, it was one of the last things we shot. People ask me why Rick would keep a big electric whisk in his wardrobe, and the funny thing is I really did have that in my wardrobe. A few years ago the rents went up and I was planning to move, I got as far as packing a lot of stuff in boxes, but then I just couldn't bring myself to leave the old place... It doesn't work now, the whisk, it's all gummed up with fake blood. That's not still Jimmy in the suit there, when Rick throws the mutant out of the window, that's just the empty suit. And now - yeah, that's me! I play the guy down on the street who gets a severed mutant eyeball in his cup of coffee. That kind of humour is one of my favourite things about Goddard's work.

Now we see the Police Commissioner's death, over in the old factory. Fed into a meat-grinder while still alive. Wow. That's meant to be his pancreas falling out there, none of us really knew what a pancreas looks likes, not even Rod, my special effects guy, so we just guessed and - oh, and now back to Rick and Liz. They've got to a police station, but the cultists have followed them. Evan asked me, where would Rich have learnt those martial arts moves if he'd just spent his life studying old holy texts and stuff? Well, maybe he spent some time in the Far East after college, or something.

Here's where Rick finally goes to bed with Liz. They're both very battered and bruised after the fight in the police station, so they're tender with each other. As before, Rick's bedroom is really my bedroom, and, uh, his bed is really my bed. Don't worry, I put clean sheets on, ha ha! Of course both the actors were wearing what's called a 'modesty patch'. Some more wonderful acting here. Rick and Liz have only known each other for a week but it's, uh, it's as if they've been waiting for this moment for years. We spent a long time shooting this scene, because I wanted it to be perfect. And also I suppose because we shot them in a lot of different positions.

The day we shot this was actually, uh, the last day Audrey spent on set. She checked into a hotel that night and flew back to Sacramento the next day. In the end I suppose it was because of - what do they call it? - creative differences. If we'd known she was leaving we would have had a party for her or something, I know the crew all loved her. We'd got some Chinese takeout and we were talking about the scene we filmed that day, the love scene, and I was, uh, talking about the characters of Liz and Rick, and how right it was for them, and, uh, you know, how it wouldn't make any sense if they didn't, I mean, if, uh, because, not that the, uh, the... You go through life and you experience certain... Whether it's mutants, or, uh... And I told hera little more about the original draft of Autumn's Redemption, and some of the things that Rick says to Liz which I had to cut out. And she, uh, she didn't agree with everything that I... Everything about those characters. And I said, well, they're my characters, ha ha! And she said, but they're not - I mean, but we're not... Uh... And I said, didn't she think that was a great scene that we shot that day, and she said... Uh, and she said... Howard, she said... And I said, but wasn't it a great scene, and didn't she... And hadn't she read the ending to the script, where the monster dies and Rick and Liz end up together, that was the movie's ending at that time, and, uh...

The crew made fun of me and Steph a lot because of her staying at my apartment that night, ha ha, but of course they were just kidding around. Of course there wasn't any... After Audrey left I called Stephanie and I told her I had a spare bedroom now, and how there was no point her getting up early to drive to the shoot when she could just, you know, be there, and how then we would have some time to really talk about what she needed to work on about her part. As it turned out she only stayed that one night, because I live in a noisy neighbourhood and she had trouble sleeping, and also she said it was, uh, kind of weird having all those cameras set up around the bed. I don't even know why I'm talking about this, I know no one believed any of those rumours, they weren't even rumours, they were just... It's all part of the - what's the word? - uh, camaraderie on movie sets. There's a camaraderie. So people make jokes like that. Just that day I remember joking with Jimmy about how he'd already slept with all the make-up artists, ha ha! You know, Los Angeles can be a lonely town.

Okay, a lot happened while I was talking there... We're coming to the climax of the movie now. Rick and Liz are in the cult's underground headquarters, and as you can see Rick's picking the lock to get into the main shrine. And now, finally, Liz comes face to face with the enormous pile of human guts sculpted into her own image. It's like her, but at the same time it's kind of wrong. And made from other people's entrails. Scary! We spent a lot of money on that. Liz wants to run away, but Rick stops her - but then the monster, which again is, uh, Jimmy, shambles out from behind his bride - the cultists rush in - a racoon looks sort of surprised - Rick takes out his gun and starts firing. Awesome. As I think I said, the original ending to City of Innards was very different to the one we shot. Originally, Rick was going to hide a bomb inside the monster's meat-woman, so the monster gets blown up when it tries to mate, and all the catacombs fall down, killing the cultists and the mutants. Then Rick and Liz escape up to the surface, and we see them driving away from Los Angeles together. But I rewrote the ending pretty much at the last minute, because, uh, I thought it would fit the tone of the movie better. So this here's the new ending. Rick agrees to give up the fight against evil and join the cult and use his knowledge of ancient mystic texts to help them take over the world. He gives in. And now Liz - you know, I just couldn't decide what I wanted to happen to the Liz character. For a while, I thought maybe the monster should eat her. Or maybe the giant effigy of her should fall over and she should get crushed by a cascade of bowels. And then I thought, maybe the audience will be too attached to her character, maybe she shouldn't die. So she was going to become, uh, a concubine for the cult leader. Or maybe just a plaything for all the mutants. But that still seemed too harsh... So I thought maybe she could just escape and live happily ever after. But that felt kind of unfair, because, you know, here's Rick, he's given up, he's working for these bastards, he's probably going to spend the rest of his life building fake people out of offal, when all he wants to do is be with Liz. And she goes off and leaves him and probably finds another big-shot guy. Is that fair? Is that fair? No, it's not fucking fair.

So that's the reason for this scene at the end here. A lot of people didn't like it. I don't know if Audrey liked it, I haven't heard from her, since, uh... Liz is in the kitchen with a guy. He's good-looking. They're happy together. They're making hamburgers. But she turns her back, and he goes over to the pile of mince on the table, and... yeah, look at that, he starts kneading it into a tiny little woman. He's from the cult! Fade to black. Because I thought, she may look for someone to replace Rick - well, not replace him, I suppose, because she didn't even care about him enough to go back and save him - who knows, he probably ends up fucking the meat-woman, a fake Liz is better than no Liz - she may look for someone to be the kind of, uh, you know, what Rick should have been to her, but what is she going to find? Is she going to be happy? Come on, this is Los Angeles. Yeah, she leaves, of course she leaves, but for what? This is Los Angeles. This is...

Uh, I don't really have anything else to say about my movie. I can't remember what typeface these credits are in. Like I said, there's a lot of material from the early drafts that I had to take out, and I sometimes think that maybe there's still a movie to be made from that stuff. But I've talked to some people at some studios about it, and they say a movie like that has to be, you know, inspirational and uplifting and, uh, feel-good. And what I like about horror movies is that a lot of the great horror movies don't have happy endings. Me and Dave always used to stay up late in the apartment drinking beer and watching horror movies on cable. And we saw a lot. And they don't have to have happy endings. The audience always expects one - I was expecting this movie to have a happy ending and I was the writer, ha ha! - but they don't always get it. So I think I'll carry on making horror movies, for as long as they let me. Just to reassure my fans, ha ha!

Well, I've been Howard Benitz. I hope you enjoyed City of Innards.

I don't know how long I have to carry on talking. I don't know if

Transcript ends

joanna benecke

Boiling Water

Roughly eight minutes after the alarm clock had begun its first set of beep-beeps Mr. Norris oozed from the sheets and reflected, as he did every weekday morning, that in under fourteen hours he would be back in bed, Diazepam swallowed, disappearing into a comforting, rotating haze. Of course, it hadn't always been Diazepam. There had even been periods when soporific substances weren't necessary, but, as orphan Annie and Daddy Warbucks so cheerfully sing, "that's, not now, that's then!" Of course, Mr. Norris could not watch the film version of Annie without wanting to tear the heroine's carrot-coloured wig off and insert it down her wind-pipe, yet whenever he and his wife babysat her grandchildren he would suggest watching Annie. He remembered taking his daughter Jane to see it at a West End cinema many years ago. Neither of them had enjoyed the outing much. Jane was sulky and wanted to know why she couldn't have been named Annie. "I don't want to be a plain Jane," she had said. "Your mother chose your name," Mr. Norris had replied.

In the kitchen Mr. Norris turned on the radio. A male voice was singing, "below those blue hills, dear, this time, you'll never grow out of fear". Mr. Norris flicked the stereo's switch back to TAPE. Sitting down at the kitchen table he noticed that EL2's commentaries on Wilfred Owen's – Wilfred Owen's what? The title of the poem escaped him. That line about honey yet for tea was all his brain would produce when he keyed in 'poets of the Great War'. And he knew that was Rupert Brooke. Rupert – was that right? Or was it Robert? He stared at the essays, which were just far away enough to be illegible without his glasses, and realised he didn't want to be reminded of Owen's title. What had originally attracted his attention to the heap of hand-written sheets was the dark, mushy stain in the top left-hand corner of the first page. By its size, and gooey, pus-like nature Mr. Norris could guess that it would already have seeped through more than ten pages. A few years ago this would have pleased him. He had enjoyed being the mad Englishman, the untidy genius-eccentric who spilled Bovril and Marmite on crisp, white Scandinavian essays. He had even, though only occasionally, purposely placed a perspiring mug of tea on a piece of homework – no, assignment, the language of international schools invariably being American – anticipating the giggles of his students' end-of-class conversations, "Check out this shit on my assignment! He's so crazy". He had enjoyed the adrenaline rush of overhearing himself described as "One of a kind kinda guy, yeah? He's got this whole English shit going on, it's cool."

But that's, not now, that's then.

He looked at the new kettle which he had bought the day before after carefully comparing different makes and models on the internet. The chosen 'water boiler', as the Scandinavians chose to call it, was made of frosted blue plastic with a clear strip of plexiglass running vertically along each side to allow the kettle-owner to watch the water begin its slow waltz which gradually built into a climactic, a-rhythmic jive. The memory of the satisfaction Mr. Norris had felt, as he plugged his new kitchen appliance into the wall the previous day, wearied him this morning. The kettle saddened him. A single night in his kitchen had deprived it of its independent glamour, its glossy integrity. The thought of his wife waking in an hour or two and molesting the kettle further made him queasy. She had recently lost some weight with the help of a book by Dr. Atkinson – whose heart had exploded – and even the skin of her hands sagged somewhat. He revelled in the devastating vision of these folds of skin unconsciously spanking the blue plastic as she shoved her fingers under the lid to open it.

Should he take the kettle with him?

He could keep it in his car, perched serenely on the passenger seat; or maybe he should return it to the sterile aisle in the sterile shop where he had found it? But then there was the hassle of boiling water in a saucepan to be faced. He had to accept the facts: the kettle would be corrupted.

He loved his wife, though they hadn't married for love. Twenty years ago she had attended a conference in Southampton and seen him karaokeing 'Pennies From Heaven' in a pub. Both emerging as cooling lumps from burnt-out marriages, unable to face hearing of their ex's new lovers from within the solitude of a meal for one, they got married. At the time Mr. Norris was teaching at a comprehensive where a student had recently disposed of a foetus in a lavatory; the chip-shop opposite his flat had food-poisoned him twice in the last month; and Jane had refused to see him since the divorce. She had moved with her mother to Bristol. Or was it Brighton? There was no reason for him not to settle in Norway.

His wife's name was Gunn – pronounced 'gun' – a retired social worker with lumbago. Usually he did not resent her much, but recently, whenever she spoke, her words seemed to fly sharply from her and pierce his throat. It was as if she was shoving something small and hard into him, pressing and pressing, just below his Adam's apple. He couldn't speak, could hardly breathe, in her presence. Especially since the Death of The Novel.

Mr. Norris had begun The Novel to revenge himself on the teacher who had told him that English was not a proper academic subject, when, a bright eighteen year old with floppy hair, he had filled out his university applications. During three dull years of Economics (culminating in a disappointingly low upper-second class degree and IOUs to a mushroom man in Camden) and the following one of PGCE, Mr. Norris buoyed himself along with the thought of The Novel which would fucking well fucking show everyone. Unlike the majority of those who live this cliché, Mr. Norris had actually got some literary talent and over the years The Novel had developed. Exceedingly slowly, it was true, but now, some forty years after its conception, the end could finally be glimpsed. Then something happened. "You'll never grow out of fear, you'll never grow out of fear". The song of the moment. And the title of The Novel.

The first time he'd heard the song Mr. Norris had variously tried to convince himself that it went "you'll never get out of here," "you'll never go out, I fear," and finally, with the creativity born of desperation, "you'll never grow a green beard". But eventually he had been forced to accept that the title he had mused over for near on half a century was the same one that four American teenagers had chosen for their punk-rock anthem. Mr. Norris couldn't quite explain to himself why this bizarre, but hardly earth-shattering, coincidence had made him cry.

The Novel wasn't a novel anymore; Mr. Norris had fed it page by page to the old kettle, pausing every ten pages or so to flick the switch to ON and watch a few water-logged years waltz and jive, before pouring the pulped fiction out of the window. The kettle had given up on page 547 so he had chucked the remaining sheets out with the lifeless water boiler, deleted all the files on his computer pertaining to You'll Never Grow Out of Fear, and searched through the kitchen drawers until he found some drawing pins.

Later that evening Gunn told him she thought it was a real shame that he'd given up on The Novel. Her Scandinavian accent annoyed him intensely: "it iz a riil scheym"; each word pressing, pressing below his Adam's apple. Leaving the room, Mr. Norris stuck a drawing pin in his thigh. Then he stuck one in his chest, which hurt a lot more.

That was then.

Now, a week later, Mr. Norris had his new blue kettle and several packets of drawing pins. He had inserted a pin into each of the chicken breasts residing in the freezer, which he hoped Gunn would prepare when her son came over for lunch that day. If you twist the needle off a short drawing pin it is possible to insert it into a jelly baby without noticeably altering its outward appearance in any way. This discovery kept Mr. Norris company as he drove to school, leaving the kettle ready for his wife to use.

Nick Mohammed

Good

My birth came as such a surprise to all those heavily involved. A gun shooting out of the end of a bullet I recall being the most feverish and most unlikely of metaphorical hyper-jargon. Straight out of my then mother's cosy, handmade womb – no strings attached…kind of.
"What's that for?" I quizzed. She gobbled it up quickly before I had time to ask; "great quiz," I cootchie cooed. I never expected that of a virgin.

So that was how it all began back then: an interesting concept. My early years were spent shedding my yolk and tale to become yet another spermèd egg to add to my collection. This is well documented, has never been questioned and is taken as faith, although it never rang entirely true on odd occasion, for want of a phrase. "Where's Daddy?" I mentioned politely one whoring. "Never ask me questions like that ever again" said the Virgin, as if something really deep and meaningful was toying with her virgin mind. I presumed she was worried that he might have an accident at work and plane off his face. I respected her for that and resumed sucking on her teats. Today was a Sabbath, a day of zest and (obviously) teats.

It turned out that being human being had its figments of my imagination, but all the same I studied hard at it for a while and continued to do things such as lunch, language and age. Until one day an oh-so tiny Godly voice spoke a little louder please into my not-so-oh-so tiny then eye, now larger-than-life ear (it turned out). "Listen," it smelt, "I feel you're good. You're meant to be sharing this you little devil!"

And so that was how it all began again. Rather like, I say 'tomato': you say 'allergic', He said: "Go get 'em kid!" I said (rather sillyly) "Papa?" (Apart from back then it was all in Hebrew). "Hide!" shouted and interrupted the Virgin strangely suddenly, "Joseph's back!" I stood where I was and noted how plain, simple and miraculously uncomplicated it was for His omnipresence to dissolve into nothingness – as if transparent air between no sheets of glass had melted into the purest of watery ghostlike crystallised emptiness. Mary was used to it (and the use of jargon) and looked thoroughly unimpressed. Just then, Joseph waltzed in the room singing something I now swear was sixteenth century (Note: I can only reconsider this in hindsight and so my memory is/was a little fuzzy). Mary continued to pretend to gut a cow, cursing under her breath – something indefinitely heathen. Regardless, I felt – at that very moment – a surge of overwhelming power hurtling towards me at break-neck speeds. I had no chance of avoidance in accordance with the Scriptures: I'd been spotted since Christmas and was quite frankly overwhelmed. "Merry Christmas" cried Santa from some distant and foreign land, "not yet" I retorted blandly, as he continued to vomit something wholly tasteless in my immature opinion.

I decided that now was the time to start lying down some rules. The term: "What do you want: a miracle?" refers to basically saying "No, there's not a chance on God's Earth or in hell we can afford to get you another donkey, monkey". (I added the 'monkey' bit on myself). Later I found out that they would make similar and less convoluted statements as: "He's even walking into wine: how odd". I was getting really good! Finally things were starting to make some kind of sense.

As luck would have it, I was taken to see lots of people that day. Within their place I healed five, wounded six and ate four. "That's fifteen," I giggled, "and not entirely true". I was right: I ate eight: ("nineteen," I slobbered). It made me think though: less eating and more healing would have been a good thing...or at least an example of a good thing. I just had to stop being such a greedy pig! Jesus Christ!

Gradually my number of followers doubled. I noted that not once did I ever do things by halves apart from when I did them twice and that was only once I can recall right now. One too many good deeds in those days counted for more than your life was worth. Obviously it was well worth mine in the end, but all the same you had to be careful.

I got to my careful feet, crossed my heart and hoped to die before leaving that day. I'd never been so frantic in my life: this was going to be a good day! "Don't forget to look your best" said mother, as I combed her long, virginal hair. I plaited her into my beard as soon as she said this and left for the desert. It seemed years since I'd been there last week...although it turned out it was only forty days, which became just over a month.

The cheeky devil had gone to huge extents to make my sandy-stay more than welcome. But I had conjured up a dynamic and an unnecessarily huge resistance to enjoying myself (especially that day it would concur) and was merely bored by the whole ostensible ordeal. The haphazard-apple-trap snake (for want of a lord) didn't say much apart from a brief discussion on whatever, which I attempted to ignore despite my boredom. I was genuinely getting rather hot and can't say that I wasn't overtly surprised when I delicately plucked three feathers from between her crotch. I think that I thought it was time to bread back – my temptation was being watched like a hawk, I noted. Hawks eats snakes… and who the hell was her crotch? I'd never been allowed to arouse such thoughts in the past and assumed it was the work of the sexy devil's horn…definitely time to bled back.

It suddenly struck me that I was going to be late. He didn't say it was going to take a whole three days. Three days of that, forty nights of this – twelve days of Christmas…I can't quite say that it wasn't just Da Vinci and I who were surprised and intrigued by the considerably paradoxical numeracy at play here. Presumably one day, a populist novelist will pick up on this and its ties avec countless descriptions of beautifully French artwork…perhapsérment.

On a practical note, my ordeal was far less challenging than I'd anticipated. Everyone had shown up and I welcomed their howls of laughter; their sheds of tears and their general nods of concealed approval. Some were blatantly clock-watching. "Any time now," one would spout, as if for his own sake. (If it wasn't for my sake none of them would be there, particularly later on in life). I finally graced them with my presence and have allegedly been there ever since, though sometimes I wake and redeem them of such beyond belief.

My death came as such a surprise to all those heavily involved. "Good heavens!" I cry from above. And they always – rest assured – answer back.

Michael Ledger-Lomas

The Sleeping Faun

He pondered the Sleeping Faun. Massive beneath its cupola, it was still as creamy and light as the ices from Gunter's at the wedding breakfast, which had so quickly melted in the hot reception room. His tongue flexed sadly behind his teeth as he recalled the cooling bath each mouthful had been. The Faun flowed over its knotty couch, a single drop of grey flesh splashed to earth. Its eyelids were tightly but languorously shut. Its fists had flowered open after some unknown exertion. Its haunches, once stiffly propped, were now relaxed in what was sleep or an approach to death. He moved closer to where the great shining chest barrelled up against the ivy trunk. His fingers coiled around his Handbuch and tightly pressed its red morocco covers. There was a gentle sough that he felt but did not hear as its thin leaves layered together and fused. His stock rasped his chin as he let his gaze sweep and his head twitch up and down over this wounded and seductive beast. Then suddenly her voice came, an irruption into the calm.

"Charles. I really think that you might leave that now."

"My dear. Of course. I thought that you had been happy to wait for me, as usual, under the portico."

"Believe me Charles, I am ordinarily so much more comfortable there than roaming around these scraps of-" her gaze pointed beyond his hip, to where the Faun's goaty foot is sprawled at ease- "of- the Antique. And yet I must tell you Charles that it is becoming impossible for me as a lady to be left to dawdle there alone. The passing men are quite unmannerly. I almost believed that I was to be- accosted." She would have dabbed her eye at this, but he was still involved with his marble and she decided to economise on the gesture and raise her voice instead. "They are so drowned in their beer as to forget common decency. I begin to find fault, really, that you should desert me all day for this-"

"It is a faun, Henrietta. You are of course quite right. Come, we shall go for refreshment." The Reverend Charles Bromhead looped his arm through that of his wife of two months and a day. They passed as stately as the statues that crowded in on them back through the gallery, past the sneezy ushers and out onto the steps of the Glypothek. The Munich sunshine, still angling off the Königsplatz and into their faces, briefly stalled them. Then they moved away from the gallery portico, inching their way down what were steps for titans. Bromhead's boots creaked as they manoeuvred carefully around Henrietta's flounces, which lapped the flags. They moved off towards Odeonsplatz. Their walk had that deliberative, tripping pace that announced to similarly circumstanced passers-by that they had wealth and leisure enough not to need to go quicker. They passed small knots of ambling Franciscans at whom Bromhead cordially scowled, peasant women with bright handkerchiefs knotted around their brows. Then there were the officers.

"Look, Charles dear, at that soldier. His waist is laced up as tightly as the silliest of Belgravia girls! What good should a dandy like that be in war?"

Bromhead's eyes travelled skittishly over the bright tunic, the carriage belt that pressed as severely against a stomach as a stay, the thighs poured into tight breeches that flowed into the shiny boots.

"Doubtless, Henrietta. But he certainly looks to have conquered you. Please be so good as to avoid such an- an immodest inspection. Now shall you be happy with Tambosi's?"

Bromhead looked around as if to secure a line of retreat back to his marble halls. His ears filled with the drawling Bayerisch of other strollers and the sound of a barrel organ coughing out Auber. Henrietta's officer chatted with a girl obviously fresh from the Victual Market but perhaps, imagined Bromhead, more in the habit of selling herself than Wurst or cheese. Bromhead thought it his duty to quell the man with a gaze but in doing so met his eyes. The officer curled a moustachio as if he were dangerously amused to be hauled before a clergyman's stare. The colour of his eyes was unclear at the distance, but perhaps they had a devilish glitter? Bromhead's own fancy irritated him. It savoured of Bulwer-Lytton, something Henrietta might say. He turned and swept her on to the Café more rapidly than her shoes allowed; he felt chastened by her complaints.

Bromhead had been surprised to salvage anything of their stay in Munich from the disaster of its first evening. It had been late afternoon when they had arrived at the Gasthaus. They had crawled slowly across Europe in the last three weeks, spurning the still imperfect railways for the creaking diligence Bromhead's father had left him. During all that time he was aware that he had yet to honour all the pledges he had given on that early summer's morning, at St George's, Hanover Square. Nightly they had lain awake and apart in stifling pensions, their minds following a droning mosquito's track or startled from rest by the explosion of a drunken song from below. By day, the diligence itself had enforced their separateness. Henrietta had been inside, tapping an idle finger against the pane, deep in the second volume of Clara Fitzpatrick: a tale of Irish life. Bromhead had preferred to mount the box, pretending to exercise his French in conversation with the coachman. But after assaying a few remarks on the weather and a carefully turned commonplace from Corneille or Fenelon, he would lapse into silence and stare moodily at the landscape, as he would at an unconvincing diorama.

Until they had arrived at Munich then, Bromhead had not found the right moment to encompass the thing. He had hoped that things might go differently there. A sense of natural shyness might be alleviated as they settled into the pleasant sense that their home was made for the next month or so. His curate had assured him that the Gasthaus presented cleanliness, respectability and moderate charges combined. That one could imagine oneself to be in an English inn. He would lay out his folios and his leather bound notebooks. Henrietta could finally slip the locks on all the cases, change out of her travelling dresses and make a start at properly inhabiting her married self.

The way to the Gasthaus was slow and involved. The diligence had crawled through a dense tangle of lanes and beer cellars, the whole so very different to the Athens in the Alps that Bromhead had fondly imagined. It was perhaps eight by the time that they had taken their supper and the whirlpool of snuffy old porters and red armed maids had spun from their rooms, leaving them alone. Bromhead shuddered mildly now when he recalled what followed, just as had on the hot July days that began their stay, when a sweat drop hatched under his curls slipped down his neck and under his collar. Though it was nine and the curtains closed, the rooms had seemed altogether too light. Not that he had wanted the hymeneal rite to be something viewless. A man had a duty to prize his

wife's nakedness during it, not to go to it in blackness. Yet Bromhead had somehow imagined that he would be engaged in this during one of Mr Tennyson's decorous twilights; an English summer evening with choirs of birds bringing their gifts of pure song. Instead there was this sepia gloom, guaranteed only by the gimcrack curtains. A clock ticked insolently and every few minutes they had heard a muted "Grüß Gott" from the parlour below, which the floorboards could not fully muffle. He would remember the startling whiteness of her neck and how her head had lolled meekly to the side, like a St Catharine ready for the final blow. He found the sheets and her shifts fused together in dampness and mildly adhesive to her thighs. The porcelain shepherdess by the clock leaned hard on her crook as Bromhead had struggled from his check trousers. Henrietta's sighing had been continuous, sending up to him a telegraph of mingled warning and invitation. He had looked away as he embarked on a trembling push, up at the dark patch on the faded wallpaper discovered when they had scolded the maid into removing the print of the Jungfrau.
Later, as he lay wincing into his pillow, uneasily conscious of her sobbing, he had taken comfort from the reflection that tomorrow he was at last to see the Sleeping Faun, which he had hitherto known only from prints.

Charles Bromhead had left England the toast of Mayfair. With the Crimean war at its height and the first wounded men already home and limping in the Parks, he had issued David's Lays and National Duties, showing in prose and verse that the Psalms spoke of the truth of our cause. His little chapel had filled with ladies whose fear for their men folk seeped easily into admiration for this bright paladin, clad in the breastplate of hope. The Hon. Henrietta Symonds was one who had strayed within the crook of his dauntless arm for protection. She chose to remain there as his wife. Bromhead had been hard put to explain both to her and especially to others why they were to spend the lion's part of their honeymoon in Munich. No, he had explained over tea to the Dowager Duchess of Westmeath, they were not sure whether they should even cross the Alps. Would the Reverend not then take his bride to Italy, not even for a peep at Milan or for Christmas at Rome? Bromhead thought not. It was all very- freethinking of him, quite a heresy against Mr Murray and Herr Baedeker. Bromhead was glad that his heresies strayed no further in these unsettled times. But what was there to keep a man for so long at Munich, wondered the retired Admiral. Was Bromhead running after these painters they had read of in the Quarterly? Or maybe, hey, it was not Helicon that he had a thirst for but all that beer? Bromhead had deliberately sipped the Dowager's weak tea. Well it was neither. Perhaps the Admiral had read of the Glypothek and of the princely collections of antique art it contained? Bromhead meditated a work that would bequeath him an unrivalled reputation as a champion for Christianity. He would demonstrate to the satisfaction of the learned world- not to mention the elegant world, simpered the Duchess- that Greek art gestured to something Higher and Truer than itself. Surely its plastic quality contained something 'legibly divine', heathendom's unconscious witness to our coming redemption?

The party had fallen into a muteness they could not break. The Admiral, unable to scratch his head in mixed company, contented himself with a grimace. In the hall way a footman coughed. Bromhead had looked around and brokenly finished his speech with the observation that, in particular, there was to be observed there- that there was a Faun. The Admiral thought that Bromhead had been drinking a little too deep with Mr Ruskin, what? He must pardon them if he seemed a deal too aesthetical for such simple folks as they were. Bromhead summoned up the smile that had first earned and then sustained his pew rents. No doubt the Admiral was right. In truth, the brainwork of David's Lays had left him quite over-taxed. He should go just to please his fancy, recuperate his Greek and practice his German.

Day following day after that first night he had fled to the Glypothek to study his faun, evading the riddle Henrietta had set and which he had been unable to answer, as if it had been a corrupt couplet defying emendation. She would remain in the Gasthaus reading or join a party to sketch an Alp. In the early evening, her carriage would venture out for the museum to collect him and Bromhead's calm was at an end, for he heard unspoken reproaches in her every remark. He knew peace only in contemplation of this - lewd thing, as Henrietta called it. He saw no lewdness in it, but a beautiful prophecy of the Deposition. He could spend hours before it on his little camp stool, cross referencing its profane curves with others he found in the vast Handbuch der Kunst that was his prop and alibi. In time the art students who drifted through the

Glypothek to sketch a hand or a foot came to know him, greeting his appearance among each other with a broad grin and to his face with carefully assembled English remarks. Among one another they spoke of the Herr Pygmalion, who was short-sighted enough not to have chosen a nymph to contemplate. Bromhead disapproved when he heard their laughter echoing through the galleries. He had read about German students, these fascinating young men with their open collars and thick beards. Guilty of so many a moral lapse and red republican in their politics. He would look at how the faun's neck splayed back- so like the Christ, so like- and imagine it bearded or think of his own return to Mayfair with a set of fine moustachios and how the Dowager Duchess might shriek. Then he would blush deeply at his dreams.

The first week of September had come, but offered no respite from the heat. Wasps, glutted on beer, invaded the Gasthaus rooms, offering themselves in dreamy sacrifice to the maid's brisk swatter. Henrietta's illustrated papers curled and yellowed on tables and against the carpet until the ladies in the fashion prints looked as ancient as Mr Layard's gods from Nineveh. Ink dried on the neck of Bromhead's bottles until it broke off in dark clots and lay on his study table like picked scabs. Henrietta sat in the velvet against which her maid advised her and watched the sky darken. It was now too late for the opera she had been promised. Bromhead came in at last from his work. His collar was askew and he carried a pile of sketches whose thick, frantic lines were like the first and rejected draft of a confession.

"You know, Charles, that this must be the ounce that breaks the camel's back. I am to understand, am I, that your nasty students come before our engagements?"

"Henrietta- you know that it is my work comes first."

"Nonsense Charles, the vile smell of tobacco is all about you."

"Well, is it so very wrong for me to move among the young men here? Their ideas are far from our Mayfair notions and yet they seem to me vastly instructive."

"I like to think that your pride might once have scorned the pleasure of chattering with German dreamers in a low pothouse. You have lost yourself here Charles, lost yourself and perhaps me into the bargain. I suppose you know that I am already cut from many excursions here and no wonder. What is one to do at the Tegernsee with an unwanted wife?"

Bromhead reached out for the desk, willing his rising sense of constraint down through his hands and into the pile of papers he had cast down. The room smelt strongly of the chamber pot. It was the odour of the street and they had tried to close their windows against it but in vain.

"My dear, - I beg you- I ask you to leave this."

"You told us yourself, Charles, in David's lays, we cannot always be in flight from our responsibilities. Up from the soft couch and its involving draperies and face the stern proof." Bromhead took gloved finger and thumb, yellowed along its length but baldly smooth where the tips had rubbed against marble, and squeezed his lips hard.

"That is - my view. But we were agreed that my constitution demanded some rest from care. I cannot apologise for caprice when it is caprice that I need!"

"I do believe Charles that your whole life is becoming a flight from care."

"Henrietta, that is entirely unjust. A man of my…."

"A man?'"

The slap Charles gave her was surprisingly dull in sound. He had never struck anyone before. It was not like the gay allegro of thumps when undergraduates had fought with the bargees at Oxford and he had stood by, flushed with excitement but unwilling to take part in such unChristian recreation. Then again, it had been sufficient to knock her down, unless Henrietta too had eked out his effort in the interests of the drama. Her bombazine skirts whooshed gently, a disappointingly gentle accompaniment to her fall. A silence. In the street below, someone whistled Rossini. Bromhead felt that he had stumbled into the Italian Opera. Henrietta raises three fingers to press her cheek and lips, as he had once seen Malibran do. He appraised her trembling grace with giddy detachment.

"You have added cruelty to your neglect. I will leave this room, sir, and call the houseboy to pack my things. In the morning I shall return immediately to London and make your conduct known there."

Bromhead could not prevent her flight. He was wordless, lacking even a syllable as emphatic as the angry rustle of her skirts as she fled the room. He was conquered by terror just when manly courses might have averted disaster. Slumped in an easy chair, his eyes closed and his mind raced to picture crowds of heads, all gravely nodding, all frowning and mouthing their regret. So terrible it had been; a mariage blanc; there was talk of ill-treatment; the father looked for redress and had insulted him in Piccadilly; the man was absolutely pressed to give up his chapel and go away from London. He jumped up to the window, peeled off his gloves and pressed his palms against the panes, making them creak in their cheap setting, sighing at the contact with their momentary coolness. He sprang at the bookcase, took up his Epistles and rifled it for a friendly text, but his eye alighted only on the good that was not in us and thorns and briars that were to be burned. In his eagerness he cut a finger on the corner of a page and a trace of blood started over the bumpy letters. When he heard a corroborative rumble of cases in the next room, he wept.

Bromhead's bad end was a favourite theme for some years to come at the Legation, though only after the ladies were installed upstairs at tea. They said, said the under-secretary, that she had wanted a satyr, while his interests ran entirely to fauns. There was always a good deal of guarded laughter. The under-secretary was a witty man; and this generally passed for wit.

jow lindsay

from The Tragedy of Beyoncé Knowles

Chapter 1

Huh? There is one trustworthy throng of dust – and though my unfounded fondness should be cause enough for a "what! ho! friend or foe?" a "stand!" and "who goes there?" and coup de "hail the queen!" – the lads are singing snatches so sweetly that I pour out my heart to them. I tell them that I love a lady, but have only an inkling what one is. Torture chamber choir, I confide, I have also been made with a more sinister impulse – a vast fear, which is like a blazing light behind me. I cannot look into it but it would spasm me to some unexamined lofty action, more crammed with consequences than a snooker cue.

My tirade – which I believe is a form of time, rather than a happening procuring a duration – so the urgency is as it always was – sprouts my first a posteriori (Lat. lit. "asshole's dream"), that the doom crooners have been advising me all along. I strain to hear them.

Pump it up!

Pump up the beats, noir choir! That's it – I make it out – they sing, "sing . . . ! sing . . . ! sing . . . ! sing . . . ! sing . . . !"

Thanks guys.

I unpack my options like a picnic basket, cursing with each low tupperware something I have forgot – the fork, the salt, the hill, its soft green grass, the tender cobalt firmament, all streaky as Kamapua'a bacon.

These are all I can find:

> Pedal to the metal – right on!
> Go wild – please read chapter 1000.
> Snip snip – please read chapter 2000.
> Phat sinner – please read chapter 3000.

Chapter 2

In a three bedroom semi-detached house in North London, tucked away from the commotion of the kebab shops and grotty pubs, yet slyly adjacent to the Piccadilly line, Dad waited for risotto. Ten minutes, ten minutes. To the shadowy attic study, prey on the PC.

The evening had come on him fast. He peered out at the streetlamps. They poured purity uselessly on dog poo. The chimney stacks were dark this twilight, a sign of Spring coming on. Here and there, short Turkish men with moustaches stood around in groups of four. If Arsenal scored, he would hear of it.

Dad drew the curtain and a chair, and tinkered with his software settings to substitute – for the tinkles and clunks of minor border adjustment or button-tickles – human screaming, incited by inhuman malice, and fastidiously documented by, well, what was left to call it? Eight minutes then. What else? Water. Bah. Whiskey. Pah, little left and so he should spare it. Love. Pah, she was in Manchester. The poet John M. Bennett (whose recent clusters of paired words conjured his hermeneutic choir like nothing since Keats). Mmm.

> Gas ket
>
> Nab 'n. t rool sofa where, you d
> rove 'n p low
> ah seal ant tasteless like a cube!
>
> Br ick
>
> Neck smear, g h aze term inus tem
> prature an mort
> are this you can? was foaming worth?

Sixish minutes.

Chapter 3

Dad's own ground-breaking prose style had cost him his job in merchant banking. He had almost satisfactorily pressed his case for dynamic tenselessness, but a fine-motor misjudgement in the clinching moments had liberated a piece of froth, a modest one, one which might have been ignored by a fellow with fibre and some understanding of posh protocol, one which had arced like tracer fire and slid beneath his employer's crashing eyelid portcullis like Indiana Jones or any number of lively escapees: "Not on projected EBITDA! . . . Now you will have to leave!"

Some of my dad's points:
- what was was co-opted by nostalgia, and thence by sentimental political autism;
- what will be shalt similarly receive hysteric theatrical toothlessness from a marketplace of competing prophecies; and
- what is is enticed into the school-side car of the immediate and the eternal but is found split and pitted on the craggy bed of the merely anecdotal.

To which:

"Not on projected EBITDA! Not on historical EBITDA! Not on meeting minutes! Now you will have to leave!"

"Spit in my eye," Dad had said.

Four minutes now. Enough to blow his fucking brains out if he'd had the foresight to procure a piece. Had he had the foresight? No. Five now. Ah. That was happening again.

Chapter 4

That version adapted from Dad's journal. Just before he died, he told me a very different story: racism. He was fired for that.

My mother and father were robustly married but my mother had not been to Manchester. Not once in her life. Was my father a dirty racist? Or a dirty cheat? Or was he clean?

I clicked the X and closed Dad's journal. A girl begged in German for her life.

Chapter 5

Between Dad getting fired, and Dad dying, Tamburlaine came to stay.

Tamburlaine, who once appropriated the many stars, moons and fir trees of my mother's cookie-cutters for the purpose of devising bullets along their lines, characteristically found solace in haggled smut and for days at a time slapped a soup of unborn melancholics across the builder's crack cleavages of many thin women. But he knocked frantically at my door, leaving a trail of wounded on a Christmas theme, and not a small galaxy of corpses spurting fountains from their new star-shaped maws. He beat on the door. I opened it and he beat on me and I on him. "Solace! As – yl – um!"

I solaced my unrequited love of milky puddings by devouring very many, spoon by spoon I did it, left corrugated containers strewn. Otherwise emotionally I was pretty solid. But I was huge, huge, I'd die of it.

Tamburlaine was emotionally a mess and thin, thin. His very words blocked his throat, and we had to slap him on the back with a piece of thread, or jab him in the ribs with two cochleal bones, or he would die of it. We took turns, my mother and I. I would speak with Tamburlaine: "What's up, shitbag? You sleep okay?" and my mother would stand by, her red whip spooled, her fingers creased around the bloody gut of a pig's ear.

"Ka! Not blah! Bad, Fuck Spag! Face!.. Infact – ah – ah – suh –"

"It's not loosening," yells Mother.

"Use your finger Mum" I say. "Be not firm!"

Mother says she is for murdering him with a hammer.

"Poke it from him gently, as if bringing a moth to orgasm."

I chose my taxonomy with care. Had I selected an ant, a cricket, a slug, a snail, a spider, Mother would certainly have thrust his lungs shut in the shameful potency of that lust. But a moth! She was tentative all right. Never such a ginger jab outside of county cricket. "Famously listless," Tamburlaine yielded, and the affectation turned into a vomit, a very light thing, akin to a line of spiderweb overgrown with moss.

Tamburlaine was not gay, but his dimensions specified penis as his pussy of choice. Before we met those girls for coffee, a week after Dad died, Tamburlaine had scored only once – at my eleventh birthday party, slipping his member into Spaz Steve's urethra and sliding towards his chambers like a snake seeking a nest of wren eggs.

My mother's definitive fuck-up was letting me grow up too fast, but whilst trying to deny Tamburlaine sanctuary she fucked up here and there, and he probed the weak points like a newborn's skull and carved in his initials, swiftly set up shop. I had bunkbeds, so that was okay. I liked to sleep on the top.

Chapter 6

A day after my birthday party, I found a message in a bottle which I didn't understand. Then I found another scrap of paper on the living room which I didn't understand:

> I have a yong suster
> Fer beyond the se
> Many be the druries
> That she sendeth me

Dad was sitting mending his gun. I showed him the second scrap of paper.

"Maybe someone brought a poem to your party," he said.

"It's ripped off," I agreed, "a big piece."

"Then let's hope the poem got to the hospital in time!" Dad said, and roared with laughter.

Chapter 7

Dad didn't notice Tamburlaine, his eyesight wasn't good.
Why did Dad lose his job?
What was his job?
Why did he lie?
Why was he he dead?

It was heavy being eleven. Mum was hardly ever home now, working on her new case, not caring about Dad. That made me angry. I'd sit on the chair in the dim room for a bit. Then I'd think I wasn't even good enough to sit on the chair any more. I'd call out to Tamburlaine with a fear, hoping he'd come sit with me, but Tamburlaine would answer from beneath the chair beside me, a low moan. So that wouldn't help.

I told Mother she should transfer her case, that she should start thinking about Dad, but, supplicant to the contrary shoulder, cur Tamburlaine cajoled her contrariwise.

One night I went into Dad's study and read his journal. The loo washes its hands having used you. Get away, you fond thoughts, you squat, greasy and culprits, in memory-space set aside for the correct names of stuff. I put a new ribbon in the word-processor.

Pulled golden hide from my shnozz. I typed furiously, while the program still loaded, and none of my letters appeared on the screen. Then it stopped groaning and settled in and it all appeared at once, a magnum opus.

Why did my father lose his job?

Let us take a moment to examine the question. Obviously, our first task is to define who "my father" was. We may then make an account of what he lost and how he lost it during the period which we intuitively (and imprecisely) designate his dismissal. Excavating this material, we may more narrowly define my father's "job." It then only remains to transform the manner of my father's loss of his job into a gestalt causal narrative.

I will argue that there is no one reason why my father lost his job, but rather, a variety of contributing factors.

I knocked *enter* five times.

The first factor which I will examine comes from my father's diary. There he records that he was fired because of his ideology. The entry is written in a comical style and was left in places where people might read it, such as our coffee table. However, just because it makes use of literary effects does not mean that it is not based in some truth.

Just before he died, my father told me he was fired "swiftly as a neurone" because of racism. People often tell the truth (or what they strongly believe to be the truth) on their "death beds." However, we can discount this fact, because it seems unlikely that my father knew he was about to die. The reliability of this source is therefore rather doubtful.

Promising thoughts gathered in another window.

> (Different uses of 'loss'? – eg. lost confidence, lost interest, lost faith in)
> (Near-homophones: eg. Lost Prophets, lust)
> (Attempted rape? Down-sizing? Or bureaucratic error?

63

Misunderstood heroism, eg. saving the whole company?)

(Quitting? 'Passive quitting'?)

(Embezzling funds? [Feed family])

(Cats 'stranger' – or was he? Drunk – perhaps only when NOW drunk was he fired because then drunk? [When sober fired because sober???])

Chapter 8

How had he addressed Mother, in those Homeric days? "I will teach you to smile, tooth by tooth."

Chapter 9

"Hush, it will be different tonight, we'll sleep okay."

Chapter 10

How my father died. The afternoon of the day after I turned

eleven, a meteorite gashed out our flowerbed. For miles around these things were punishing Parkview, and surrounding suburbs, like Tetris pieces.

The first thing to do was wash it off, dirty thing. I rushed in, grabbed a bottle of ordinary Context-Sensitive Soap, rushed out. At first I couldn't find the Context-Sensitive Soap, but then I saw it was near a box of On The Scent, which you scattered in the air to dye fragrances. Originally used in industries in which environmental conditions had to be tightly controlled, it was now extensively used in the home, as kitchen decor and sometimes as a shimmery pink finger to point justly to a guilty anus.

The thing sizzled under the nozzle like a noodle-pan. What was it? The soap turned to toothpaste. It was a tooth. Pockets of decay you could keep a bun in. I gazed fearfully up to the tightening twilight.

Dad came up behind me, put a hand on my shoulder. "Damn son," he said. "First losing my job, now this."

"I'm sorry about your job Dad," I said.

"It's okay. How was I to know that my supervisor would overhear the racist remarks I made about the new half-caste in Finances."

"More and more racial intermixing these days, huh Pops?"

Pops shifted from foot to foot furiously. "Yeah. At least after the first Poems were born around 2015, they kept to their own kind."

"In a way, all poems are half-caste, Dad. As you know, a beautiful brilliant woman scientist obsessed with Byron's poetry wrote a computer program which correlated features of "She Walks in Beauty . . ." with erotic events. What nobody has been able to explain is how the poem got her pregnant."

"I think *I* can explain it. Now, there is a genetic –"

All of a sudden there was a tremendous crash. A huge object had killed Dad. Numb, I emptied my bottle over his remains. The soap flared into shampoo.

Heads slid along over the fence, like marbles on ice. "Hey kid, what's the matter?"

He hopped off the Street. The outer strips of the Street moved at the pace of those old people movers they used to have in airports. The next strip in moved at twice that pace, the next strip in at three times that pace, and so on. It was graded like that so you could get up to high speeds, without ever having to jump on a strip that was moving really fast relative to you. The Street was entirely paid for by the Corps, so every inch was plastered with advertising. Some guys said they liked walking all over the products, but those guys usually disappeared in the night.

". . . he's dead"

"Come to my church" and he gave me a card.

"Gotta go" he said, and, "I can see my favourite Noir House advert" and he jacked the Street pretty grunko.

I went tiredly into the house and sobbed – grief reconnaissance, not the tough stuff – through some television. A pop/jazz quartet who teetered delectably on the edge of pop/punk yet contrived forgettability played a song which I hadn't heard before, called "Unleash the Quiche."

The chorus went like this:

> chains of sex!
> and gaol of CO-ral!
> keep me in my!
> complicit pas-TOR-al:
> ee-ai-woo-ai ee-ai-woo, ee-ai-woo-ai yai yai yai. . .
> ee-ai-woo-ai ee-woo, yeah ee-ai-woo-ai yai yai . . .
> CO-ral gaol! my CO-ral gaol! ai yai yai!

with much bravura. The video went like this: in the centre of our television we see the silhouette of a guitar, lying on its side whilst we listen to its heart's produce. Our perspective orbits and we see that it is being plucked and fretted by two enormous spiders. The charming animals shew off their skill. We cut to a drum kit on a similar dusky flat and hear a tapping. A man in fiery drag bursts from the snare and begins a husky croon, the words fitted ill upon a dirge remix of the 'Happy Birthday' tune just as the beat gets underway and is joined by a mellifluous wafery base line and a heaving piano riff which must be work for fifty arachnids at the least. We cut to a shabby street in a faintly Middle-Eastern town. A door bursts open into the zooming lens, and the band run onto the street. Their eyes boggle and their maws unfasten. The singer/guitarist still wears a blonde wig and searing make-up, but greyish mud tarnishes the other three faces. The singer/guitarist is prominently bleating, "I don't want . . . your advice!" with classically trained pop-punk precision as the doors fly apart, then he proceeds into the street with a flagrant lament. The band are clutching their instruments but not playing them. The drummer holds only his sticks, although the beat's filigree pulsation, and the wreckage we recently have seen wreaked upon this man's vocational tools, strongly suggests him to be only a figurehead for digital production treachery. The piano player seems to be grasping a swaddled infant, but a crafty camera swerve displays the black and white piano keys wrapped up in and leaking from his bundle. They stare in pantomimesque fear at the sky, where B52s flock joyfully. Their bomb bays open but yield only a single brown hen's egg each. The villagers below, whited and yolked, wave vengefully at the sky. We cut to the cockpit of a bomber. Uncannily, it is the band who are piloting the plane, giving one another and the viewer thumbs-ups and slapping one another's backs. Here, the first instance of the chorus. ("Chains of sex!" etc.) The pianist opens a bottle of champagne which ejaculates over all of them and the dazzling dashboard. After the champagne the video picks up speed and loses coherency. A number of tales are apparently interwoven but are but actually irretrievably entangled because the same four faces star in them all. There is a literal take on Spaghetti Western featuring an unusual Jacuzzi, which I think very stupid. After three minutes, a brief cut to the spiders, who are sexually engaged, and the village, where the villagers all are dead, their skulls pierced by fragments of egg shell. The blood trickling from the singer/guitarist's mouth mixes with the yolk and spells "The End."

    They were a political band but I had forgotten their name. The next song, which had been played unremittingly since Tuesday, was set partly on a desert island. Beyoncé, the late successful R&B solo artist, wriggled and with frequent glances over-shoulder I rubbed myself hard. A switch to a night-time urban setting, and Beyoncé folded up and dropped clumsily. By all evidence and accounts this was the real footage of Beyoncé's death by sniper while filming the video. The track was filled out with an all-star tribute, over a heavily remixed beat slapped with an almost angelic choral straightjacket. It featured Sean Paul, Kelly Rowland and Michelle Williams, worth serious suspicion in Mother's opinion.

    I remembered Beyoncé muddling cause and effect. She said she wouldn't get naked but she'd wear a bikini if it were a beach scene. (This in an interview somewhere).

Chapter 11

Mother let me grow up too fast.

Like candles in a glass, we must melt our heads to make a muck to stand upright in. The orgy I'd gleaned from Asterix and Obelix – reclining, grapes, laurels, whole boars, up to their armpits in bed-sheets.

Mother's vision – FLASH! – the guttural choir, the stench!, Christ the fucking illegal depravity. A jigsaw but unfussy. Anyone got a mouth going spare? Who farted or enthused where anal? Blast, I have come, lost interest, at the bottom of the heap with several commitments. Unprotected gatecrashers whoop. Yet I fell in love among this. Perhaps that was my only real problem with it all.

Mother, hesitantly, "Are you sure you're old enough for an orgy . . ."

"Duh Mum, duh"

Mother may have been uneasy. Tam actually scoffed at me. For four years running the weak buffoon had been a practitioner and proponent of the two-phase birthday party. After common words of baskets and eggs, he proceeded to recommend 'day' phases generated directly out of the imagery of his metaphor. For example, he suggested an afternoon of bowling (begging at gutters for more eggs, I thought, and was repulsed) or paint-ball (putting all your eggs in guns). His mental processes were laid so plainly before me that I rejected them simply because I understood them, without bothering to come up with the same things by a more hidden way.

When the day came, we played orgiastic de-individuation. We put on Tupac, dressed in goat skins, and hundreds of people first got to touch each other's thingies when we smeared them with spermicide and sweet food, and drugs to be absorbed orally and vaginally and as suppositories.

"The Dionysian throng can dance higher than any creature, because it can thrust a separate heart into each leg. Its shriek of fear coincides exactly with its most artful speech, its hideous gasp of pain on every point resembles its most delicate love lyric. Some distinctions which the abominable hamony does not observe are:

> Subjective / objective
> Self / other
> Pleasure / pain
> Torture / sexual intercourse
> Redemption / crucifixion
> Delight / mercy
> Anal / oral
> Sorcery / licking"

As the bass boomed, balloons burst, symbolising within a few yards of our eyes the annihilation of distinct bubbles of consciousness into what was more like soup. My membrane gave up the ghost. I felt it rupture and my holy offal slide into tributaries of tributaries, as if a compromise between a bee swarm through a halo and a swan through a gloryhole. We were putting all our yolks in one mighty, iron-clad egg at the centre of the universe.

But I snagged on the branches of Love – of a familiar, self-seeking, Western kind, jerry-rigged by old Arabs and taught a think or two by both Madonnas – and when the torrent lightened, I lay still a single person, transfixed and tattered on its sharp bark.

My face had been one with floral floor at the time, but I had felt her or him – brushed a toe, a little toe I think. It was O God! enough, it was like the finest point of clitoris nestled in a mammoth malicious origami of flesh.

It was a mysterious toe too, not on the guest list, and not witnessed among the dazed regroupers.

I will say 'She': 'she or he' is a stylistic sore-spot, grammatically if not sexually ('they', I pray, will be available to my children's children).

I gathered my pieces together, showered and wept, got dressed. I was eleven!

I opened my presents, but they were all kids' stuff.

leo shtutin

Here be dragons

Softly and lamentably he scribbled the letters by the flickering candlelight, softly, softly, penstroke by inkwet penstroke, and suddenly no more the pen and no more the paper and no more the candle, and in their place the infernal machine, the primum mobile of our world, the computer, and he typed softly and lamentably the letters in the still and electric light, in the harsh and electric light, keystroke by bonedry keystroke, and stopped.

What are these roots that clutch, the jaws that snatch and bite, he thought, what are these claws, these claws that no son of man can know or speak of, what is this allusion, why the confusion it creates, and what state of mind must I have to create such a monstrosity, such an oddity, and where is the sense of humour, where the bile, the passion, the style, the suffering, the cross-image, the stern and didactic form, the nineteenth century dislike for realism, the nineteenth century dislike for idealism, where is Caliban's reflection, and what were his intentions anyway?

From the third to the first he sways, I sway, I stay, I walk, I talk, I sneeze, I breeze through this conundrum, this tympanum of word-forms, of linguistic games, within the bounds of my tongue and without it, within the wake and without it, in sleep, in repose, upon my feet and above them, beyond them, through every river-journey in the world and every city, every conurbation, every quote, reference, citation, allusion, and admission to the fold, to the free house, the stone house, the public house, the temple, the red cross and the black one, and who are you fooling, they know it all already, or they don't, and it doesn't matter, I'm only repeating myself, repeating humanity, and a grief ago I read somewhere that I'm only repeating myself, that it's all been done, that this era is the era of parasites, of ticks and leeches, I hope you choke on this, take what you want and go, I don't need it anymore, for this is the era of parasites, feeding off each other, the blood still warm and red and suddenly bruised and blue, I hope you choke on this, your allusion, your parody, you're a bloody joke yourself, you know that, don't you, and yet you persist, insist on it, you say that it is the order of things, that it is the way things are, and that there could never be any other way, no ray of original and best sunlight here, just the still and electric light, keystroke by bonedry keystroke, just the harsh and electric light, and let us all reproduce, for this is the era of parasites, this is the era of information, this is the era of the tick and of the leech.

My speech sickens me now, induces me to be he, to be the third and not the first, to find some wordcover, some shelter from the harsh first, from the admissive, permissive first, from the invasive first, and my rhymed thirst for the fold grows, his thirst, I should say, he should say, he should tell me to say, my thirst grows, my thirst, but he should not yet plunge into these seas, for they are waters dark and deep, and contain much that is unknown, much that is uncharted, unaccounted for, and where is his respite, where the full stop to put a damn dyke on his verbal flow, to quell this explosive undertow, to stop his throng of mixed metaphor, double or nothing, sir, I'm sorry, I quit, these conditions are just intolerable, my insurance simply doesn't cover them, what are these, dark ages, where the sages of my time, of my space, of my place in the world, and if there be dragons, I have not yet found them, and I have still to sow my dragonseed and build an army of monsters, and an army of parasites, feeding off one flesh, and will the stench of faculties remain in the remnants of my brain after they are finished with me?

But this is deception all, angst, depression, and her thrall, if not too loud, be sweet and merry and complete, and I love, and am loved, and talk, and am talked to, in all the actives and middles and the passives and the lilacs and tulips and roses of the cruellest April, the best and most beautiful April, a year to the day after birth and death and beginning and end, and here, too, is the beauty, the power and the glory, and here my and his respite from the darkness and paranoia and the infinitely happy sadness of his daily life, from which he may enter into the boundlessly sad happiness of her arms and slender wrists, her milkwhite temples and winedark eyes, across the windblown sea I make my journey homewards, to my Dublin, to my Ithaca, to my end.

Where have I been taken, sitting here by the harsh and electric light, sitting here by flickering candlelight, my words inkwet and bonedry, into the army of hate, into the arms of love, into the slender wrists and fingers of love, into the despair of the desert, onto the harsh bed of bones, into the stone house and public house and free house, and through our era of parasites I see a reflection, a distortion in the mirror of my words, the wound dealt by the point of my vorpal blade, a serious one indeed, though not fatal, and here comes the liberating conclusion, but it is here already, and already it has passed in shades of lilac and tulip and rose over the misty mountains and far away into the distance, but she remains, and I remain, and grief remains, ago and now and in posterity, and so too does the birthjoy of love, and the world is and was and will be in that moment my sister and my mother and my daughter, and in that moment I am and was and shall be the ancestor and offspring of all my race, the father of my own grandfather and the son of my grandson, through her, because of her and not despite, and not in spite but in bliss, and if I miss everything else I will have missed nothing at all.

This precipice, this canyon, this void, it is nothing, nothing at all, and everything is in order, everything is settled down, everything settled down, and he returned, calmly, to more prosaic tones, to more formulaic shades and hues, and he was calm, and he was burning, and he was cool, and he was on fire, and he typed and scribbled, and the breeze outside the window played on the windchimes, and he felt the soft pulse of the night, the gentle tide of the night, around him, swaying gently to and fro, and dancing on the table tops and between the leaves of his books, and the memory of her smell was mingled with the smell of the night, with the smell of the wind and of the rain, and the night air lightly enveloped him in its cloak, as the clock moved into the early hours of the morning.

Ben Morgan

Threesome

I'd better start with a short description of my situation, otherwise none of the following will make sense. At twenty eight years old, I cohabit with a happily married couple. Sometimes it surprises me that I am not also in a marriage, happy or otherwise. I haven't ever been in a marriage. I haven't even come close. I'd like to ask someone if this is normal for a person of twenty-eight, but asking David and Susan, the couple I live with, would embarrass them. And everyone else I know works in the sex industry, so their opinion on this subject is of questionable value.

Currently I'm filming a movie. I forget what it's called. I think it has the word Antics in the title, but that's about all I can remember. The director is French, middle-aged, and apparently good-natured. He lent me a cigarette before the first take, even though we're not supposed to smoke because the others may not like the smell.

The other man in the movie is running his tongue up my leg. I moan. The moan is genuine, a good sign. But it's hard to stay focussed on the matter at hand when you've done it so often. At first you're so overwhelmed by the reality of doing it for a living that you live every moment of it with great intensity; but I've reached the stage where my thoughts try anythingthey can to find their way out of the same extreme repetitions.

I think about David and Susan, the couple I live with, and their little boy, Saul. I should stress that living with Saul is unlike living with your average nine-year-old. As well as having an artistic side – he's a superb musician – he's good at useful things like maths and computing. Brilliant, in fact. One teacher used the word genius at his last parents' evening, according to David, who is a proud father. Susan is more modest. She glows quietly.

Sometimes living with Saul, much as I like him, gets me down. I know it's invidious to draw comparisons, but we sleep in adjacent rooms and I'm only human.

At night I wake up from bad dreams in which David and Susan

discover what I'm really doing and order me out of the house. As liberals, they have, inevitably, a low view of what I do for a living. Susan once told me she thought pornography was demeaning, both to the performers and the customers. "Some things shouldn't be looked at," she said. I decided not to argue; she might have wondered why.

The man on top of me pulls my face into his neck, the toned muscles shifting around underneath his hot skin.

The really tricky thing is, despite my frank envy of him, I like Saul. I give him piggy-back rides and read him bed-time stories. He seems to like me as well. It is important to me, for reasons I choose not to examine too closely, that the child should look up to me. Sometimes I think it's because I remember being a child, and I'm conscious that children lack all charity. Children consider themselves and their families perfect, and pass judgement accordingly.

In this assumption, I should add, Saul is more justified than most. I have never known a marriage stronger and more harmonious than David and Susan's. Neither of them is under any illusions about the other person's limitations. David knows that Susan is neurotic, obsessive, claustrophobically locked in an internal drama connected with her father's early abandonment. Susan knows that David, forever in the shadow of his illustrious older brother, is emotionally needy in surprising ways – like a little boy running to mummy after a football match. What I'm trying to say, I suppose, is that David and Susan's perfection is not the perfection of inhuman flawlessness, but the more remarkable perfection of compromise.

The man on top of me is extraordinarily beautiful. He has high cheekbones and large dark eyes beneath a mane of glossy black hair. I make gasping noises as he enters me. I feel as though a huge force is lifting me up and turning me round and round in its hands, dandling me.

"Cut," Edouard the director says. It's hard to stop. We slow, groaning, then the man rolls off me. I think his name is Brian.

Edouard says, "That's great, that's fine. Bruce, why don't you kiss Daniel full on the mouth and flip him over?"

"OK," says the man whose name is actually Bruce. I can't believe that's what he's really called. I want to ask him, but the cameras are running again and he's tonguing my mouth unexpectedly hard. Perhaps, I think, he really likes me.

I imagine bringing him back to the house. In my imagination, they are sitting at their pretty rosewood dining table when Bruce and I walk in. David stands up, shakes Bruce's hand, claps him on the back. Susan smiles with her usual cool flirtatiousness.

"How did you meet?" Susan asks us.

"In a movie called Locker-Room Antics," I explain, suddenly remembering the title.

I visualise her face.

David and Susan think I'm out at proper acting auditions all day. I once did a soap advert which means they take me seriously, sort of.

Bruce pushes me roughly on to my stomach and I call out a scripted "Oh Jesus," but I actually mean it. I've been doing this for two years and nevertheless Bruce is turning me on in a genuine way. Having the cameras here even feels like an intrusion on something intimate.

As we climb towards our separate orgasms, Edouard keeps calling out commands. When he told us he was a hands-on director, I took it as a joke. But in fact he often steps out from behind the camera and shifts Bruce's body around, to ensure better angles. At one point he calls out, "Don't just suck it, love it." He's full of these obscene little platitudes, each one uttered with the solemnity of a priest. "You don't need words to tell a good story," he tells us during the tea break. "Bodies – that's what it's all about."

As we drink our tea, I ask him how he got into making movies. He says he began as an actor. At fifty, he's still fit, his blue eyes twinkling, his shoulders broad. I picture him as a young man: the jock, the boy next door.

In the scene we film after the break, I am changing out of my bulky baseball clothes and stepping into the shower. Bruce joins me. He congratulates me on my performance.

"Thanks man," I say.

"You looked good out there," he says, mock-punching my arm.

"Hey man, you too," I say.

"Have you been working out?" he asks.

"Yeah," I grunt.

I notice that Bruce is making the mistake of trying to inject his lines with real feeling. I wonder if he's a proper actor making money on the side. He's twenty-three, twenty-four, a bit younger than me. I feel sorry for him. Although it's not scripted, when he grabs me I move my hand along his cheekbone, a tender gesture.

Edouard calls out, "Soap," and we start to work the water on our bodies into a lather.

I wonder how I'll explain my wet hair to Susan when I get back. She's likely to be tense anyway, since David has been away for a couple of weeks. They both get edgy when they're apart from one another for too long. I remember a flight from Philadelphia to LA with David during which he talked about Susan the whole time: her anxieties, her difficult childhood, her newfound peace of mind, following their marriage.

The first time I met Susan, at one of the rubber-chicken postgraduate conferences we were both attending in those days, I found myself talking about how easy it would be for any of us, given the right combination of circumstances, to go crazy, a favourite subject for Susan, who has co-written an anthropological study of madness. I recognised that David's gentle, almost helpless honesty would satisfy her proclaimed wish for someone authentic, someone who was 'just themselves.' So I engineered a meeting.

I didn't expect to benefit so much out of the arrangement. They make good money, the neighbourhood is pretty, and the peace and quiet suit me. I've been lucky. If they only offered me their attic room out of pity, mingled, perhaps, with gratitude, so be it.

When we've finished filming the scene, I get us some drinks from the vending machine.

"I'm surprised I haven't heard more about Edouard," I say, handing Bruce his coke. "He's good."

Bruce sends me a flash of his blue eyes. "He hasn't been on the scene for a while."

"Do you know each other?"

"I live with him," Bruce unexpectedly replies.

"Since when?"

"Since I was just out of high school."

I picture the younger Bruce as a waif, a lost boy in need of daddy. I have a brief, startling vision of my own father, smoking his after-dinner cigarette and instructing me to stay at college and then get a decent job.

"Does he do much of this stuff?"

Bruce looks uneasy. "He took some time out."

There are only two reasons why a director in this business takes time out. One is that they think they can get into some other kind of directing. The other – more common – reason is that they have legal trouble. It happens often. Directors discover, too late, that their young performers are, in fact, children. Sometimes they protest, but more often they turn a blind eye, thinking of their careers.

Bruce says, "It was a while back. He regrets it."

I find the story tawdry – the schoolboy shacked up with the disgraced old hack – and, even worse, tedious. But Bruce retains enough of his glamour for me to offer him my number after we're done, not expecting him to take it.

He moves his hand though his hair in a visual cliché I find unexpectedly charming. "Sure," he says, but I don't expect to hear from him. There's a joke in the business – get everything up but your hopes – so I put Bruce out of my mind and go home.

When I get back, Susan is sitting at the kitchen table, drinking a cup of coffee and staring out of the window.

"You look nice," I tell her. She's wearing a white chiffon dress which shows off her tan shoulders.

She doesn't answer. Either she's thinking about work, or she's missing David.

"How's the office?" I ask.

"I didn't go in," she says.

"Did you phone?"

"Yes."

"What did you say you had?"

"Food poisoning."

I put my arm around her shoulders. "What is it?"

"He took an extra ten days in New York."

"Well, I guess he had to."

"To get some papers signed? Really?"

I sigh.

"There's this girl," she says. "She works for the bank out there."

"How many times have you met her?"

"Three, maybe four."

"And why do you think —"

"I'm not saying it's necessarily happening."

"So what are you worried about?"

"She's got amazing legs. I know it sounds stupid. But you know David and legs. The other night she wore a gold lamé thing that would have been ridiculous on anyone else, but because her legs are so amazing it looked great. And she's twenty-six. She told us: 'People think you can't do a job like this when you're only twenty-six.' I saw David's face, he was really impressed."

"Susan, that means nothing. Also, I don't know 'David and legs.'"

I often think it's done Susan no favours to grow up beautiful, brilliant and rich. She's never had the safety net of her own ordinariness the way the rest of us have. I'm also conscious that these fits are partly performances, done for her own amusement and mine, ways of playing the neurotic wife, of keeping the role at arm's length.

"I met a guy today," I say, changing the subject.

"Oh, yes?"

"He's called Bruce."

"What is he, a trucker?"

"No, he's an actor."

"Tell me it's Bruce Willis."

"It's Bruce Willis."

"Then I'm proud of you."

The room is filled with sun. Plates, fridge, sideboard, floorboards glimmer in it like clear water. The sunlight in Los Angeles is unlike any other sunlight I've ever seen. It's as if it strips away impurities, sheers everything to the bone.

"Daniel," Susan suddenly says. "I've been thinking."

"Probably a mistake."

She ignores this. "It's time you went back."

"Went back where?"

"To university. You could stay here for a while, go to UCLA."

My mouth goes dry. "But Susan," I say, "I don't want to."

She sighs, looks at me. She has the air of someone who is about to spit something out. "Let's face it," she says. "You're twenty-eight. This whole acting thing – well, the most important thing is that you gave it a go. That's what really matters."

"I'm still …"

"You're bright, Daniel. Better than that, you're brilliant. I meet people every day who aren't fit to tie your shoelaces and you're sitting around doing nothing with your life."

This isn't the first time Susan has gestured at this subject. She's temperamentally incapable of subtlety, so I was already aware that she – and therefore, probably, David – have been thinking about it. I've even prepared an answer.

"Susan," I say, "If I'm under your feet here, I'll go elsewhere. I don't want to be eighty years old and living in your granny flat."

Susan gets up from the table and puts her arms around me.

"We both love you," she says. "We want you to be happy. We want you to do what you're good at, Daniel."

I'm so angry I can hardly speak.

"Thanks," I say, move her aside, and go up to my room. Sitting on the bed, knotting and unknotting my fingers like I used to do when I was on my own as a kid, I think about what Susan has said. I'm not clear why it has provoked me so intensely. Sure, it's galling to be given advice by one's more successful friends. But this is different. It's stronger, crueller.

"I'm going out," I call to Susan as I walk out of the front door, and close it without waiting for a reply.

The dusk has given the beach a warm golden glow. As I get nearer, I can make out, as usual, the men and women of staggering beauty who spend their days strolling up and down the beach. One man throws me a look, but I don't respond. I want to get to the water. The heat and the light coming off all the walking bodies make me feel oddly nervous.

I have a weird rash that keeps rising on my left leg. It's back again. I don't want to get sand in it. As I immerse myself in the sea, it prickles and jabs, but in a strangely pleasurable way. I dive. Slowing, quietening, the light caresses my eyes. Everything down here is calmer. It's as if sleep were a place you could enter with your eyes open.

Strangely, the distorting water gives everything a half-familiar shape. I could almost mistake a row of pebbles, glimpsed out of the corner of my eye, for Susan's face. The rock on my left takes on the features of my father. He is frowning. I see myself at eight, alone and frightened on the corner of the football pitch; bright and loud at twelve, in front of the class; at sixteen, confused in a club somewhere in Boston, letting a man called Johnny run his hand up my thigh; at twenty-three, in a library, bored, trying to write about the beauty of Mesoamerican art, while privately concluding that beauty is not something you write about, but something you touch.

After a few minutes, I get out of the water and lie in the last of the sun, drying. I allow my mind to empty itself of its images, like a tipped cup.

When I get back, Saul is home from school. He shows me the prize he's won, for maths. It's a textbook called The Numbers Carousel.

"What's a carousel?" he asks me.

"It's something that goes round and round," I say.

"I thought they were called rides."

"A carousel is a kind of ride," I tell him, and pat his head. He goes back to his seat at table, where he is eating some kind of candy. "Can I help with the dinner?" I ask Susan, another peace offering.

But she's frosty. "Everything's under control," she says.

"Look," I say, "I'm sorry about earlier."

"We'll talk about this after dinner," Susan says. That's not a good sign. That means Saul's dinner, which means she doesn't want to talk in front of him because she's got nothing nice to say.

When Saul's gone, she says, "This can't go on."

"What can't?"

"David and I have done everything we can to get you back on your feet. We want to help you. That's all we've ever wanted. But you can't expect us to support you, emotionally and practically, doing something which we all know is bad for you."

"Susan, I'm happy to move. I've enjoyed being here, but if the time has come for me to move on, I understand completely. I've always been very grateful, as you know, for everything you've done for me. But don't give to me and ask me to alter myself in return."

She throws up her hands, a characteristic gesture. "I'm not asking you to alter yourself, for Christ's sake. If anything, I'm asking you to be yourself. When I remember how you were when I met you, and see you now —"

"I was bored, Susan. I didn't feel I was getting anywhere."

"And now? What are you getting to now?"

"Something I've dreamed about since I was a kid. There's no way of predicting what will happen, I admit that. And if that's a problem for you, I'm sorry. We'll go our separate ways."

Susan starts stacking the plates in the dishwasher. I move to help her, but she waves me away. As she inserts each plate she allows it to knock piercingly against the bottom of the washer. With her back turned to me, she says, "You know what, Daniel? I don't believe you. You're not living out a childhood dream. You're just acting like a child. The reason you turned your back on teaching to make beans commercials was that you knew that you'd be good at being a teacher, you could succeed at it. But that raised the stakes, didn't it? That meant you had to work. So you backed off. You chickened out, Daniel. I find that pathetic. In fact, I find it worse than pathetic. I find it contemptible."

I realise we have reached that dangerous point in an argument where it's becoming possible to say unforgivable things. The most dangerous aspect of that kind of row, of course, is how much fun it is at the time.

With an access of adrenaline headier than anything I've been experiencing recently I say, "By 'acting like a child', do you mean acting like Saul?"

Susan stops stacking the dishwasher and looks at me. "What?"

"Well, when you call me childish, I just wonder if you know what you're talking about. Christ, your own child isn't childish. I've given him a nickname, in fact. I call him the BoyBot. Can't you just see the slogans – 'Wonder of the World, Only Nine years Old, the Perfect brain inside a miniature Bank Manager!'" I pause for breath, delighted, briefly, by my own viciousness. "But then, you've never been childish, have you, Susan? You've been waiting to be forty-five years old, with a good career and a mortgage, since you were about six. And I've seen photos of David when he was a kid, with his little black combination briefcase which he should have got the shit kicked out of him for and probably did. In fact, all of you are so buttoned up I'm surprised you haven't choked."

Buoyed up by the fluency and violence of this little speech, I walk out of the house. In the front garden, Saul is playing with a toy truck. His pale little face peers at me. He's heard the raised voices, I can tell. He stretches out his hand, and, against my better judgement, I take it.

"Can we go to the beach?" he says.

"Sure," I say. "I was heading there anyway."

Hand in hand, we walk down the street. The afternoon sun is dimming a little, shadows unfolding around the houses. Saul says, "Why are you and mummy angry?"

"We're not really angry," I say.

"Mummy says you need to grow up," says Saul in the cool, mechanical voice children reserve for taboo subjects. He's staring at the ground.

It's no good, the fury's back. "Do you know the word fuck, Saul?" I say.

He turns his blue eyes on me in surprise, giggles, but doesn't reply.

"Well, your mummy can go fuck herself," I say carefully.

I don't know where these aberrations come from. It's obvious that, if I'm to maintain any kind of friendship with David and Susan, I very seriously need to have them less often, but they arise so unexpectedly.

To my surprise, Saul doesn't run away or burst into tears. Instead he just goes quiet and continues to trot along next to me.

Soon, we are getting close to the beach. In an attempt to bring things back to normal, I say, "Why don't we build a sandcastle?" Saul nods mutely. We find a space on the sand a little way down from the lifeguards and start to dig.

I ask Saul how his music lessons are going. I've heard that he's doing well on the violin, and his singing voice has been described by his teachers as "beautifully controlled," or so David told me.

He says, "Not bad. We're doing Schubert."

"Wonderful," I say, trying to sound authoritative.

I wish I hadn't just said fuck to Saul. In fact, I wish it so strongly that I feel on the verge of tears, or of kneeling before the child and begging for forgiveness. In their sheer theatricality, I suppose these impulses are childish, or at best, adolescent. But since children supposedly don't feel shame, and I'm overcome with it, the feeling is paradoxically reassuring.

Eventually, Saul and I have cleared a reasonable space in the sand, and begin to shape it into a kind of mound. For a long time, we're quiet. Then, suddenly, Saul speaks, so quietly I can hardly make it out.

I stop kneading the sand and look at him. He is looking down at the floor, motionless.

"What did you just say, Saul?"

He doesn't reply. There's a pause. Then he looks up at me. "Daniel, what's a darn fine BJ?" he says in the same mechanical voice, looking pale and serious.

I sit back on my heels and take a deep breath.

"Who said that word to you, Saul?" I say, trying to smile reassuringly. I'm wondering if I somehow brought this all on by saying "fuck".

Saul looks down at the sandcastle. I was wrong, of course, about children feeling no shame. He blushes profoundly and then jerks his head to the left. I find this gesture inexplicable. The silence continues. Eventually, Saul gets up and reaches out again for my hand. As we walk over, in the direction Saul glanced at, I wonder why he always needs to hold someone's hand.

"Here," Saul says, pointing at a scrubby bush at the edge of the beach. I kneel down and find a small blue object tilting outwards through the sand and the bush. I reach down into the sand and unearth it.

It's a shoebox, so full the top is almost coming off. I pull away the top and see a pile of magazines, magazines that I recognize, because I've been in most of them: January Boys, February Boys (all the way through to July), Down and Dirty, Slave Central. In among them is a copy of The Numbers Carousel.

"I already had one," Saul explains.

"What?"

"Before they gave me the prize."

"Saul," I finally say, "how did you find this?"

He says, "I just saw the box and opened it."

"When was this?"

"A few months ago."

"A few months?" I quickly swallow my outrage. It's crucial, I guess, not to give the child a guilt complex. "Well, that's fine," I say inanely. Then I add, slowly, "Saul, do you like these magazines?"

The boy blushes to the roots of his hair. "Dunno," he says, shrugging. He is leafing through one of the magazines. Instinctively, I reach out to stop him. As I do so, he looks away, out across the sea, as if trying to pretend he is somewhere else.

The magazine has fallen open at a double page spread of two cowboys, one of whom is administering, the blurb claims, a darn fine BJ to the other while they swap down-home anecdotes outside a saloon bar. One of the two cowboys is a tall, gorgeous black-haired boy of about twenty-three. The other is me.

I close the magazine, not looking at Saul. I stuff all of them back into the box and bury it under the bush, far enough down that none of the box can be seen.

I get to my feet, pull myself together. I reach down to take Saul's hand, then think better of it.

"Saul," I say carefully, disguising my nerves, "you're not going to tell mummy and daddy about this, are you?"

He fixes me with his clear cornflower gaze.

"I already did," he replies.

amir baghdadchi

The Fall of the St John-Hopkins

Whatever the masses may choose to believe, there is, in truth, no reason why one cannot combine the founding of a medical school, the saving of the third world, and the necessity of hiding out under an assumed name in a Caribbean tax-haven.

To prove it, those celebrated patrons of learning, Dr Bolchazy and Mr Hopkins, had met on the whitewashed veranda of the Hotel Paradiso, on the island of St John; and though their hands were occupied with cocktails, their minds were fixed upon the East Anglian fens.

"I don't care what you say," announced Dr Bolchazy hotly, "it is a good name. 'The Cambridge International St John-Hopkins Institute of Medical Studies'."

Mr Hopkins was unconvinced.

"Still ambiguous."

"Fine—'The Cambridge International St John-Hopkins Institute of Medical Studies, Cambridge'. That, surely, sounds like money."

"Perhaps," replied Mr Hopkins, who was admirably free from any prejudice against the rich. "But why is it that in every one of your photos, students are on little boats with that cathedral-thing in the background?"

Spread before them were freshly printed leaves of what they were both calling, with unwarranted accuracy, the 'mock prospectus'.

"That is King's College Chapel."

"The school won't be anywhere near it."

"Postally, no. Spiritually, yes."

"And that's your idea of marketing?"

"It will work! I know it will."

"Yes, well let's hope your grasp of medicine is more impressive."

Dr Bolchazy was wounded. An alumnus of one of Georgia's finest Bible colleges, he had as deep and extensive a knowledge of medicine as a doctoral thesis in theology will easily admit.

"It's only a two-year program—no qualifications necessary—I think I can handle it. Anyway," he added, "I've learned a lot by watching."

Undeniable; for Dr Bolchazy possessed ten seasons of a medical soap opera on DVD, and knew every plotline.

Mr Hopkins briefly pretended to care, and said: "I've spoken with the Minister of Health and Automobiles. The school will be chartered in St John, the curriculum approved in St John, and graduates will be only licensed to work in hospitals on St John."

"There's no hospital on St John."

Mr Hopkins waved his cocktail umbrella in a gesture that was obscure, but most likely expressed his horror at such a travesty in public health.

Of the nature and extent of Dr Bolchazy's powers of healing, some hint has been given. Mr Hopkins, in contrast, as if to complement his associate, had himself no experience in doctoring patients, but he was widely recognized in the U.S. as having doctored other things, on a grand scale. Indeed, faced with seven-to-ten years of recognition, he had chosen, purely out of modesty, to flee to the Caribbean. It was there that he was first moved by the plight of a long-neglected group: those who could afford medical school, but lacked only education, propensity, ambition, and skill. He longed to help them—to found a bold new kind of medical school, 'suited to the needs of real people in the real world'. The tuition fees, certainly, would be very real.

Mrs Choo was looking out the window of her five-bedroom, three-and-half-bathroom house in Pacifica, California; and though the day was bright and benevolent, in her heart it was dark with rancour and pain. Two months ago the Chatterjees had dared help themselves to a new Land Rover, and were parking it defiantly in her view. Next, a new mailbox, just like her own, shaped like a windmill, but with the addition of a Dutchman holding a flag—a flag meant to flap in triumph over her. Even then, Mrs Choo had remained calm. For unlike the Chatterjee girls, who were finishing high school, Mrs Choo's own daughter was set to become assistant manager at the Lickety-Split Ice Cream in the Lomita Mall; and Mrs Choo looked forward to fashioning from these cones a veritable club with which to smite the Chatterjee pretensions.

Then Mrs Chatterjee had rung. "Such good news, Connie ... the letters came today, and both girls going to Stanford! ... Oh, definitely pre-med. No question ... And how are things with yours? Enjoying her year out? Such fun, really ..."

And so Mrs Choo spent the afternoon consumed with jealousy, looking out her window, staring at the Chatterjees' door, and mentally detonating the windmill. It's not fair, she thought, and she expressed this to her husband in the strongest way she knew how.

"It's not fair," she said.

"The burning of Atlanta wasn't fair," replied Mr Choo, who in later life had become preoccupied with the fate of the Confederacy.

"This is worse. What are we going to do about Scarlett?"

"Scarlett will inherit this house and cultivate our land."

"We only have the lawn."

"Green," murmured Mr Choo; then, after a pause, "like Ireland."

That evening Mrs Choo had recourse to the only instrument a conscientious mother has in the struggle to secure a prosperous future for her child on short notice: the internet. From it she drew up a list of promising medical schools. Very quickly—perhaps she objected to the kinds of research they did—she eliminated the top ten, twenty, fifty schools; and soon after, came to the opinion that, if you really wanted to learn medicine—you know, hands-on, out-of-the-box thinking for real people in the real world—you had to do it overseas. One institution stood out, with a famous name—several, in fact, strung together in a way that would cripple Mrs Chatterjee when she saw them on her neighbour's sweatshirt. Mrs Choo filled out the application herself, and prepared to wait several weeks for an answer.

Ten seconds later, she received an email response:

Dear Cchoo218,

The world of medicine is a tough and challenging one, filled with intensive competition and challenges. Each year we are forced to turn down several applications of the the highest academic merit, out of our dedication not just to excellence, but diversity. Which is why we are pleased to offer you a place in our program this fall. Congratulations, Cchoo218! Let the healing begin!

Please click on the link below to supply bank details.

Mrs Choo hesitated. It was far away; and she would miss her daughter. Then her glance fell on the house across the street: there, in the half-light of early evening, the bastard windmill Dutchman was smirking with his little flag.

Her mind was made up. The Chatterjees must be crushed!
Scarlett was watching television in her room when her mother came in behind her. Scarlett usually couldn't be disturbed when watching television; you could certainly try; but it almost never worked.

"Scarlett? Scarlett? Turn around, honey ... No, okay, you don't have to ... um ... Good news, honey. You're going to medical school. In England."

Scarlett turned around, looked at her mother without expression for a full minute, and said:

"Wha'?"

As if conscious of its great mission and grandeur, the edifice of The Cambridge International St John-Hopkins Institute of Medical Studies, Cambridge, squatted in a business park; and the business park in turn squatted in a fen. Architecturally, it was not free of fault; for, while two stories had been planned, work on the second appeared to halt abruptly in the middle. But this only heightened its picturesqueness, especially after the gardener had covered the frontage with ivy, so that it looked (everyone said) like some ancient ruined abbey, but with parking. Taxis, rejoicing in the distance from the station, were pulling up.

"Here it is then, Miss. Thirty-six quid."

Scarlett thought about it, and blinked.

"I don't have a squid."

The man caught Scarlett's reflection in the rear view mirror. She was staring ahead blankly, and had not shifted once the entire ride.

Presently the whole lot was filled with crumpled luggage and crumpled students, none of them talking, most of them frightened, with no idea what to do next.

But then the doors of the Institute were flung open and out strode a short, muscular woman who blew on a whistle round her neck and began issuing instructions. This was Professor 'Coach' Collar, Dean of Fitness. Professor Collar wanted her old job back, and hated this one. Frankly, what was the point of teaching them medicine, when they couldn't even do pull-ups?

"Come on! Put some hot pepper in it, people! You're all late. Reception's started. Room B. Get inside. Single-file. No, leave your luggage out here."

They all marched in. Somewhat gratuitously, she used her stop watch to time them.

"Rub-bish," she thought.

Man, did the people at the St John-Hopkins know how to party. About a hundred people were there, and there were things to drink, and there was a banner, and some balloons, and there were things to eat, but the best were these tiny hotdogs in a crust. Scarlett had nine.

"Oink, oink!" said a grotesque voice, and she heard a cluster of sniggers behind her. Scarlett turned to find a pale, skinny boy with a blonde forelock, who was smacking his lips in a rude mime of her to the rapture of several onlookers.

Scarlett hated him.

She escaped to a table where they had name tags, and you could pick what colour you wanted. She picked blue. Later she looked down and saw she hadn't written anything in, and it just said 'HELLO, My Name Is —'; but when she went back to fix it, someone had stolen all the pens already.

The international flavour of the reception did not stop at the tiny hotdogs. Students had come from Macedonia, Italy, Uganda, Colombia; many Americans were there, a handful of Canadians, and a contingent of Singaporeans who dallied and darted through the crowd in unison, like a school of fish. (It was the policy of Admissions to seek ever a balance between rich and poor: for when they took students from the poorest of nations, they insisted on their coming from the richest of families.)

"I don't, I don't want to be a doctor," said Miranda Taddler, a neat, freckled English girl with a bob. "Really, I'm a journalist."

"Like at a newspaper?" asked Scarlett.

"Sort of… I just started on the East Anglia Auto Trader. Want to see a piece of mine?"

Scarlett said yes, and was presented with a one-by-two inch advert for a Ford Festiva.

"I'm sorry, I'm sorry. I know, it's rubbish. I'm rubbish."

"I like it."

Miranda brightened.

"Well, I'm going to do more than just cars."

"Like … motorcycles?"

Miranda could have died for her.

All the Faculty were there. Dr Phelenon, who was a bit of a pervert, brought a stethoscope.

"Oh, you'll do fine, I'm sure of it," purred Professor Default to Scarlett. "Tell me, how many bones are in the human body?"

"Don't know."

The doctor paused, removed his glasses, and wiped them with the air of man utterly checkmated by a superior intellect.

"Extraordinary. You got the trick question. Naturally, when a patient first comes to you, you never know for sure how many bones they have until you've ascertained the case."

Scarlett nodded.

"Indeed. Now, I was just wondering, if you couldn't perhaps loan me a tenner? Bit of a problem with payroll right now…"

But before Scarlett could answer, a shock of expectation ran through the room, as a white-coated figure grabbed hold of the podium and smiled benignly on the crowd.

"Dr Bolchazy, our Director," whispered Professor Default. "He's chairman of the World Health Association."

"Wha'?" said Scarlett.

"Precisely, the W.H.A. You've heard of it. Impressive."

This was indeed impressive. The professor himself had never been able to learn more of that excellent charitable organization beyond its name.

Dr Bolchazy gushed his address. Scarlett's mind wandered to all her luggage outside.

"...our fine Faculty, culled from the best institutions in the world..."

This was well put. Most members of the Faculty, having toiled for a generation at other schools, were ripe for the culling when Bolchazy descended upon them. Some had difficulty adjusting to the new curriculum. Rumour had it that Dr Kangkeider, for instance, was still, at heart, very much a veterinarian.

"...a Core Curriculum of Central Topics..."

Scarlett was definitely not listening now. Her luggage. What about her luggage? It was her luggage. It had her things in it. Twenty-eight issues of Pop! Miss Teen, and Fluff Weekly, to name twenty-eight. The fear had mastered Scarlett that, once she was out of America, and without constant reminders, her Torah-scholar-like knowledge of celebrities would deteriorate, and leave her unable to rejoin society. So she packed her magazines.

"...And with that, ladies and gentlemen, I say, Welcome to St Johns!"

Someone whispered to Dr Bolchazy.

"Right, sorry, we can't actually say 'St Johns', due to the threat of legal action by the University."

Everyone was streaming out now, eager to reclaim their things. Scarlett was the last to make it to the parking lot.

Her bags were missing.

"Lose something?" taunted the boy with the forelock.

"No," said Scarlett, to deny him the satisfaction.

So Scarlett went straight to Dr Bolchazy's office to report what had happened. He wasn't in. A young secretary with plump cheeks was chatting on her mobile in a voice devoid of tone. To say that she was a 'bored secretary' would be to imply that, in another context, she might have been vivacious. She would not have been. Nicky Ponder's ruling passion was a lack of one.

"...S'pose so ... Yeah ... yeah .... whatever ... what? ... no, can't hear you ... can't hear you ... can't hear you. Whatever." Nicky ended the call, noticed Scarlett, and said:

"Bad reception."

"I liked the tiny hotdog things."

Neither of them said anything for two minutes.

Presently Dr Bolchazy bounded in.

"Someone to see you, Dr Bolchazy."

"I see that, Miss Ponder."

"Just saying," drawled Nicky.

Scarlett followed him into his office in silence.

"We've been looking forward to meeting you, Miss ..." His eyes went smoothly to her name tag, but in vain.

Scarlett said nothing.

"Right, start again. Have you had time to formulate any impressions of our little institute?"

Scarlett said nothing.

"Okay. Not a talker. Not comfortable with English? Quite a common thing. Still, we take all kinds. That's our mission—that's diversity. Black, white, little, yellow, all of them." He waved a multicultural hand.

Scarlett said nothing.

"We didn't have to do it. We could have garnered the academic cream. But cream, you might've noticed, has a tendency to be white."

Here he grimaced, to illustrate this new form of lactose intolerance, but still Scarlett said nothing.

"Jesus Christ. Right, Nicky," he hollered, "you did it again. How many times have I told you, if we're going to admit chinks, at least make sure they know English, or don't let them in to see me."

Then Scarlett said: "I'm calling my mom."

But Scarlett didn't call her mom. Or the police, about her missing bags. Dr Bolchazy explained everything. It was all a mistake; she misunderstood; he took full responsibility; it was no one's fault; she shouldn't feel badly; he was still her friend. —None of which worked. And then, he mentioned something he wanted to show Scarlett—and he would show it to her if she came round the next morning. This worked.

That night she was installed in the Eurohostel, a dormitory the Institute shared with Cambridge's most undemanding language schools. She tried to pass the time with a British gossip magazine, but didn't know any of the stars. It was bitter.

The next morning Dr Bolchazy was waiting by the entrance. More specifically, he was waiting beside an open-top low-down round-hipped double-overhead camshaft fuel-injected two-litre one-thirty horsepower Italian sports car, the colour of clotted cream. Keys jingled in his hand, then Scarlett's.

"There now, just you take this out for the day, and when you come back, the whole thing'll be our little secret."

With that, he patted her head, and disappeared inside.

Those scornful of Scarlett's abilities, and doubtful of her prowess behind the wheel, prepare to be signally confuted. Because, Scarlett could drive. She could drive, and she loved to drive. Driving was her calling, and cars called out to her to drive them, fast, and faster, but she would never scratch them because, as a driver, she was perfect. She drove without fear, or flaw. On highways, on backways, on salt flats, in cul-de-sacs, on narrow strips on coastal cliffs, she sped without error, she trafficked in speed, she unclogged arteries, she coursed through the veins of a hundred cities. And as for the highway code, the California Highway Code, the most challenging in the world, she had it down, she had it aced, and she would never, under any circumstances, part with or swerve from a page, a rule, a line, a word, of any of it.

Not even the bit about driving on the right.

Nicky heard the crash from the parking lot.

"That's what I was saying ... oh, what? ... Hold on a sec ... yeah, that was a crash .... someone's probably dead."

Thoughtfully, she put down the phone and yelled out, for the sake of general information, that someone was probably dead. She then resumed talking.

Hating as he did to burden unduly the emergency services, Dr Bolchazy forbade anyone from calling 999 and scrambled to the scene himself. But upon discovering his car, nearly bisected by the tree, with Scarlett lying limp inside of it, so bitterly did the pathos seize him, he cried out, "She's ruined!"

"No, she's not," bellowed 'Coach' Collar, who was kneeling beside the driver door, attending to Scarlett. "In fact,"—and here she motioned with her stopwatch—"she's reached her target heartrate; thirty minutes of that daily, and you're on the road to good health."

They helped Scarlett out. She was stumbling, and badly shaken, and her neck hurt.

"Right, honey, we're going to take care of you inside."

"I-I think I need a doctor," moaned Scarlett

Dr Bolchazy and Coach Collar exchanged glances.

"Hey," cautioned Dr Bolchazy, "let's not go overboard."

The Institute's infirmary encouraged rapid rehabilitation. On one end was propped a high, vinyl-covered bed with sheets the weight of stationary; on the other, a corrugated metal door, which slid open to transform the room into the building's loading area. Still, Scarlett found it preferable to the Eurohostel.

A few days after the accident, she woke to voices in the corridor.

"Mr Hopkins called again."

"Did he say why?"

"The same reason he called the other six times."

"Thank you, Miss Ponder. What did you say?"

"I told him that he needn't worry because you were well on your way to securing the Red Cross endorsement."

"And what did he say to that?"

"He asked me if I was reading that off a card."

"Were you?"

"The card you gave me, yeah."

"You were supposed to memorise that."

Impervious, Miss Ponder continued.

"He also said, it was too late to back out now since he already raised funds on the back of the endorsement to fix the last thing you botched."

"Passionate man, Hopkins."

"He said I had a lovely phone manner."

Dr Bolchazy sailed into the infirmary and gave Scarlett his special 'number three smile'.

"How are we?"

"I want a tv."

"Can't have one. Can't afford the tv license."

"What's a tv license?"

"I've tried that one. Doesn't work. They still make you pay. I hate Britain."

"I'm calling my mom."

So Scarlett got a television.

A day later the boy with the forelock thrust in his head, then waved in his troupe of students, giggling at her like bacchantes.

"Go away," said Scarlett.

"She's watching 'Murder, She Wrote'!" shrieked the boy.

"I like 'Murder, She Wrote'."

"She likes 'Murder, She Wrote'!"

An atomic bomb of comedy! Everyone jeered, and then vanished in a universal chortle of triumph.

Suddenly, Miranda Taddler appeared with a rolled up copy of the East Anglia Auto Trader.

"I brought you something to read. It's my latest."

And then she disappeared in embarrassment.

Unrolling the magazine, Scarlett found a brief blurb by Miranda, about how the new Citroen had the largest trunk space of any vehicle in its class. The way it sat on her lap, the pictures and pages, recalled, distantly, her magazines; and when she thought about how she had lost them, she waited until the corridor was clear, and sobbed out loud as if that would bring them back.

In her many years with the British Red Cross, Mrs Ernestine Stipulate had parachuted into war zones; leapt from burning hospitals; interrupted executions; and stared down dictators. But this was the first time she had ever been kidnapped without her knowing it.

"I appreciate the ride from the station, Mr Bolchazy," she said as they pulled into the Institute's drive, "but I am quite certain I had arranged to be driven directly to the clinic."

"It's been an honour, ma'am, and it would be an even greater honour if you could step out with me and see for yourself the wonderful—"

"Stop trifling. The meeting begins in fifteen minutes."

"Ten minutes, ma'am, is all anyone needs to instantly appreciate the St John-Hopkins—"

"What exactly is the St John-Hopkins?"

"Just the world's only medical school suited to the real needs of real people in a real world."

"Never heard of it."

"That's because we believe in doing good without drawing attention to ourselves—unlike some other organizations."

"Like the Red Cross?"

He cursed inwardly. It had been going well so far.

"Well, what do you say, Marjorie?" asked Mrs Stipulate to the backseat.

"I need to use the loo," said little Marjorie.

Mrs Stipulate looked him in the eye with the expression she usually reserved for the most febrile dictators and duplicitous attachés.

"Ten minutes."

Fearing that Mrs Stipulate would not get the right idea from observing classes in session, Dr Bolchazy had declared a holiday for all faculty, staff and students, with a mandatory blood drive for everyone in the afternoon which, with luck, Mrs Stipulate might happen onto.

That being considered insufficiently festive, it was decided to throw a party in the same room as the blood drive. Scarlett, now recovered, was assigned the task of food and decorations. The latter were to be blown-up photos of what were supposedly the Institute's students, engaged in performing an impressive variety of medical procedures on laughing Africans. Scarlett was also given an immense banner with the Institute's logo and the motto, 'Caring for the Wretched'. She wasn't tall enough to pin it up, so she spread it like a rug on the floor.

"You're telling me," said Mrs Stipulate as they made their way to the party, "that the whole Institute has the day off for a blood drive?"

"Yes, Mrs Stipulate. Because we care."

Mrs Stipulate had a soft spot for those who bled regularly.

"Well," she said, "If half of what you say is true, Bolchazy, then I am impressed."

"Ma'am, you may see for yourself."

"I shall."

The party was a success. Dr Default spiked the punch. Dr Phelenon, who was a bit of a pervert, came in latex gloves.
Scarlett had shrewdly ordered several hundred hotdogs, and was feasting

on them with Miranda and Nicky.

They were trying to have a conversation about pirates, but kept being bothered by the sound of fake laughter emanating from the corner. It was the boy with the forelock, fluttering a page torn from something.

"What are they laughing at?"

Scarlett did not need to look twice.

They had her magazines.

The boy with a forelock waved another page and said hilariously, "What trash!"

Scarlett stormed up.

"What's wrong, want your trash back?"

"It's not trash! Give it back!"

He wouldn't.

"It's not trash! Give it back!"

He wouldn't.

"It's not trash! Give it back!"

He wouldn't.

Scarlett took a deep breath to calm herself down.

Then, she punched him.

In the first few seconds, nobody could speak. The boy, more shocked than hurt, swayed, unsure what to do, but he swayed too long and Scarlett socked him again, this time in the stomach, and he buckled. Jeers from the crowd! That was his permission, that was all he needed, and he grabbed her by the sweater and pulled her down, kicking out her legs from under her. Scarlett went to the floor, tears welling up, but then boy began to kick her, first in jest, but the cheering got louder, and no one wanted it to stop so he did it harder. That was a mistake, because there was no crying now, Scarlett twisted round and grabbed his pant leg and bit his ankle, with the intention to bite it clean off, and he howled and kicked her once more in the face, but he was already going down. By instinct he knew not to hurt her, he went out to humiliate her, and pinning back her hands he slapped her, with relish. She shoved back, they were now scuffling directly over the banner, and when Scarlett saw the chance she took the boy's forelock in her fist and with his head in the other hand she began smacking it down, again, and again, right over the word 'Caring'.

It was then that the doors opened, and in rushed little Marjorie, followed by Mrs Stipulate and the doctor.

Anyone observing Mrs Stipulate's sudden appearance would have immediately likened it to the descent of some god from the machinery, to seal the lips of discord and dispense to the feuding factions a heaven-sanctioned peace. Sadly, no one observed her.

"Mamma, they're killing each other," observed little Marjorie with relish.

Mrs Stipulate commanded them to stop at once. When they didn't, she strode over and prised them apart with a mighty hand. The boy, sensing adjudication in the air, collapsed on the ground in an attempt to appear mortally wounded.

She asked what all this was about; Scarlett told her and pointed to her magazines. Mrs Stipulate extracted one with two fingers.

"You were fighting," said a voice of pure scorn, "over this ... trash?"

So Scarlett punched her in the stomach.

Mrs Stipulate reeled slightly, but that powerful woman could take a blow of greater force with ease, and would have, had not the boy with the forelock been sprawled out right behind her, making her lose her balance and swing to the floor with a thump.

Little Marjorie screamed and bolted. Dr Bolchazy leaped in front of her. She swerved to avoid him, rammed head-on into a hospital bed, and quickly emulated her mother in measuring her length on the floor.

"Right," said Dr Bolchazy, "nobody call 999!"

"Should somebody get some meds?" said a voice, and a dozen people went scurrying.

Mrs Stipulate was reviving.

"What... happened?"

"You're going to be all right."

"Hey, look at that, she's bleeding from her head!"

"Can I get a bandage here?"

A little man ran in with a bottle and cloth, applying the latter to Mrs Stipulate.

She slumped unconscious.

"What was that!"

"Chloroform."

"Chloroform!"

"I'm just the chemistry teacher," said the little man, who began to cry.

Someone rushed in and handed a bundle to Dr Bolchazy.

"Bandages!"

"This is sanitary blue roll! We can't use that."

"The lady's wearing tights," said someone, "those are white."

"They don't have to be white!"

It was too late, they were already denuding Mrs Stipulates' calves.

"Is the girl dead?"

"Still warm!"

"I'm calling 999."

"Don't!"

"Wow, she's forming a puddle."

"Coach Collar, get them out of here! Put them in my trunk. Dump them somewhere."

"Where exactly?"

"How about Cherry Hinton?" offered someone.

"Sure thing, sir."

"Histon's good."

"It doesn't matter!"

"Is the trunk big enough?"

"The new Citroen has the largest trunk space of any vehicle in its class!"

"You can call 999 from a payphone once they're done."

Coach Collar slapped a body over each shoulder, making sure to lift with the legs.

When it was done, Dr Bolchazy said: "Thank God no one will ever hear about this."

It was perhaps the fastest-selling issue in the history of the East Anglia Auto Trader…

"MEDICAL MASSACRE … Fens Run Red With Slaughter of Innocents… the fraudulent academy of Dr 'Death' Bolchazy… students forced to fight in pits… kidnapping of secular saint … neither the pleas of bystanders nor the shrieks of a frightened child could deflect him from his murderous plan…"

And that was all it took. Of the once proud citystates in the age of Solon and Cyrus, Herodotus observes, that while it may have taken the toils of generations to found an empire, the smallest, most improbable incident could dissolve it in the space of a breath. Thus it is, sometimes, with international medical institutes.

Scarlett was among the last to leave. The police wanted her for questioning, Dr Bolchazy having somewhat inconveniently gone on leave, and the rest of the Institute having discovered the pleasures of budget air travel.

One evening, she was walking back to the Institute, when a car slowed down beside her; Dr Bolchazy was at the wheel, and Miss Ponder smoking in the back.

"I'm not running because I'm afraid," he said with spirit, "I'm doing it to shield the woman I love." Scarlett looked at Nicky, who shrugged meaninglessly.

Then they drove away.

Scarlett Choo is an assistant manager at the Lickety-Split Ice Cream in the Lomita Mall, and likes it all right.

Mrs Choo does not plan on leaving the house for several months yet.

fiona mcfarlane

The End of the World

The problem was that in the warm winter the caravan park would flood and then the sharks came nudging around the play equipment. The previous owner had rigged up a pirate's flag and spent three months writing out receipts while his ex-wife steam cleaned the sandy carpets. For this reason all the vans were moored on stilted platforms a few metres above the ground. When Ed and Selena took over the place in summer it looked like a fairground in convalescence. In their first winter, Ed called it shark fin soup. "It's like we're on a raft at sea," Selena explained to her friends. "It's like we're floating into a tropical rainstorm."

Back when Ed could cope with the smell of the sea he'd taken a photo of the whole place and they'd had it made into postcards for Selena to sell when they opened up in summer. They paid for the postcards instead of wedding photos and every card had 'The Venice of the Shoalhaven' printed in the bottom left hand corner. In the summer, when the sea had gone, Ed laid down the astroturf and people liked to sit high on their caravan steps to catch the breeze, even though it smelled like crabs. Everyone bought handfuls of those postcards and asked Selena to send them. Usually they were so happy to be on holiday they had forgotten the names of their families and Selena was expected to address them by herself.

"Put them back on sale," said Ed, who always used to have leaves in his hair and walk at a slope as if he were on a sand dune. He would spend the day driving between the vans in a small buggy that surprised children and prompted strangers to offer him beer. He carried out the maintenance work with a look of unexpected sincerity and developed freckles in the small of his back. Then he would shut the shop and lift Selena onto the counter where her bare arse left an imprint on the visitors' book. That, Selena guessed, was how she ended up pregnant every summer, and all the old women who were so bored of their grandchildren they had learnt to play bingo in foreign languages would make her iced tea and advise her on baby names. For a girl, they advised, you want the names of flowers and jewels. For a boy, just don't give a name that could also go to a dog.

Because of the old women, Ed would refuse to come near the shop, and by the winter the baby would be gone. The more this happened the more often Ed would set himself up in one of the empty caravans and wonder how he had ended up needing to row himself to the toilet. In the end he stood on his top step and pissed straight into the water until it became reasonable to him that the circling shark fins were a sign of the end of the world. That was the winter Selena noticed the baby had stayed with her and started to develop a personality. She could tell it liked the smell of vinyl because it always kicked as she re-upholstered the caravans' leatherette kitchen benches. There were no old ladies to make her iced tea so Selena continued to row herself from van to van, checking for leaks and scraping mussels off their undersides. At low tide she went prawning while the sharks waited and Ed told her to take her gumboots off before she came into his caravan.

"I've been trying to think of names that sound right for a boy or a girl," she told him while he took the heads off the prawns. He was watching the news and stopped with the prawns every now and then to take notes with a fishy biro. He had signed up with a bookmaker who took bets on the end of the world, and he liked to track the odds.

"What we want is an Asian name," said Ed, "and then no one will know the difference." This is how Selena knew he was distracted.

"There's Leslie," she said, "and Kerry, and Pat, and Gabriel."

"That's an angel's name," said Ed.

"I know. I like it." None of the prawns looked pink enough, and Selena imagined them floating around inside her.

"Well it seems just about right," said Ed. "It's going to take a miracle for that kid to ever make it."

"Don't say so," said Selena, but she was smiling because he'd started to rub her feet, even though his hands had prawn on them.

"I don't want a name that sounds like he might be a girl," said Ed. "Let's wait until it happens." On the TV screen, a rigged election caused riots and panic among the faithful. Selena knew the phone was about to ring. Someone on the other end would ask Ed if he wanted to change his bet for a small fee, and Ed would say yes. He had patiently explained to her the ways in which it was an investment and because she didn't understand figures she kept quiet. Anyway she understood the feeling of waiting for something impossible for so long you began to think it might happen.

On one afternoon Ed suspected that the end of the world had come and he wanted to call Selena into his caravan. A southerly wind had brought rain and flying fish, and the air was green with the beginning of a hailstorm. Something about the formation of the clouds worried Ed and he wished he'd quizzed Selena on her dreams earlier that day when he'd seen her sail past his window like a star of the sea. Selena wasn't answering her phone and Ed grew increasingly worried at the possibility of a final flood. When she did appear it was to save her belly from the hailstorm, which she was concerned would pockmark the baby's head. "My darling," said Ed. It was a good beginning.

The storm lasted for fifteen minutes in the furious way of storms in that part of the world. Afterwards, the caravan park was clogged with jellyfish that Ed, in a poetic mood, described as the hair of graying mermaids. Ed and Selena didn't bother to put their clothes back on and stood on the top step to survey the damage. The pink and green seaweed draped over the caravan windows gave them a festive look. It seemed unlikely that it would ever be summer again.

"Not the end of the world," said Selena.

"I should have known," said Ed, struggling to see it as a learning experience. "Something was missing."

"What about him?" asked Selena, looking at her belly, protected from hail and wind and other behaviour of the weather, from sharks and jellyfish, from splintered wood and harsh cleaning products, from all the dangers a day holds, and especially from loneliness.

Ed re-tuned the radios. Selena rowed them over from the caravans and took them back again carefully so nothing could shift the dial. He looked over the accounts for six hours straight and told her how lucky they were not to pay council tax in the winter. Then he looked out the window at the water and laughed and said "some luck". He hadn't bothered to take up the astroturf and now flaps of it emerged in the mornings like the kind of algae that changed Ed's odds when it scummed a lake in Western Australia. Selena noticed that his caravan never smelled of the sea because it was always so full of the steam his breath gave out since he started worrying too much about the end of the world. On the nights she went there to climb into his bed, Selena left the light on in her caravan so she could see it and imagine herself at home repairing the fly screens with a magnifying glass and strands of her own hair. The baby tried hard not to move on those occasions, and Selena usually felt like it had crawled away and curled itself somewhere in the top left hand side of her rib cage. Sometimes she would sing to it and then Ed might cry and ask her to stop. Afterwards he would ask her why she always smelled of vanilla. "I do it specially," she said. "I know you can't stand the smell of the sea."

It was on a night just like that she found the drowned man. She had rowed herself home, and she and the drowned man arrived at her caravan at exactly the same time. She pulled him into the boat as quickly as she could and checked for signs of life but knew straight away what had happened because his eyes looked so sad to be there. Selena was very unused to unexpected visits in the winter and wasn't sure what to do. She knew she couldn't tell Ed because it would make him bet more money on the end of the world. It seemed possible, for more than a few seconds, that she could install him in a caravan of his own, just to have him stay for a few days in a companionable way. She was, however, concerned about his influence on the baby, who had not yet encountered death and whose questions she didn't feel qualified to answer.

It was high tide and the sharks were slowly drifting past the laundry block. They followed her as she rowed to the shop where the phone rang constantly with people who had left love notes taped into the toilet cisterns. The drowned man seemed to like the shop because his eyes brightened when they saw the shape of Selena's backside on the visitors' book. The baby liked the shop too, because something moved inside Selena a bit like a muscle cramp and a little like the unfurling of wings. This happened just as she rang the emergency number and she could only remember to tell them that someone haddrowned in the Venice of the Shoalhaven.

She sat the drowned man on the deep freeze and all the iceblocks swam under the glass beneath him like sardines. She read to him from the lending library but all the books were full of sex scenes in which men cried and women smelled of vanilla. She told him that Ed had not been out of his caravan for five months and preferred now to pee out the window while standing on the leatherette kitchen bench, and she suspected that the drowned man felt sympathetic to both of them. She explained that her baby's name would do for both sexes but that for the first time she thought she really wanted a boy. When she guessed that he was embarrassed she began to plait the fishing flies into his hair, and told him that he was handsome although he wasn't. Then she found she had to sit down because the pain was too great and the water seemed to be coming into the shop now and muddying around her feet. Soon the whole sea would follow it and she wasn't sure that she could swim with whatever it was that was pulling at her belly. She could see that the drowned man had also become anxious and she found time to worry about him.

"There are people coming for you," she reassured him. "Ambulances and probably the police. They always send helicopters if somebody drowns."

Just as she said it she heard the helicopters and saw the cars pull up on the shore with all their headlights pointing over the water. Privately, she wondered about all the fuss over a man who was already dead. All Selena could hear were radios that she thought Ed must have tuned incorrectly, or maybe she had knocked them because suddenly she had become so clumsy. She took the drowned man by the hand and hoped he would move when she asked him to.

Then she called for Ed. Somehow he was at the door.

"I know," he said. "It's all right. I knew it was coming."